W9-CPN-542

"You'll never know if you can make it unless you try. But if you're afraid, I'll go back and bring a truck," Derek said beside her.

Sydney gave him a thin glare. He was the reason she felt determined to get up that snowbank that rose twice as high as her head. "And here I thought you were going to manage not to say something insulting. I am not afraid."

He lifted his hands innocently, but the devilish curl of his lips was anything but. "It was just an offer."

"I think I can manage," she told him. "*You're* not giving me a push, either," she told him under her breath.

"Didn't offer, cupcake. But if you want my hands on your butt, say the word. We don't have to like each other to want each other."

Dear Reader,

Welcome back to the world of Weaver, Wyoming, and the Double C family!

Derek Clay is a pretty traditional guy. Believes in family, duty, honor. He works hard, likes a beer and a game of pool with his cousins now and then, and can definitely appreciate a pretty woman.

Sydney Forrest isn't exactly a traditional girl. She's an heiress, for one thing. Having never experienced a particularly happy home life, she's never thought that "family" was for her. But now Sydney's in the family way, and for the benefit of her child, she's reevaluating her entire lifestyle.

His life is pretty settled, and he likes that just fine. Her life is anything *but* settled, but she thinks at least she's got a plan.

And then they meet….

Best wishes,

Allison

A WEAVER PROPOSAL

ALLISON LEIGH

If you purchased this book without a cover you should be aware that this book is stolen property. It was reported as "unsold and destroyed" to the publisher, and neither the author nor the publisher has received any payment for this "stripped book."

Recycling programs
for this product may
not exist in your area.

ISBN-13: 978-0-373-65656-1

A WEAVER PROPOSAL

Copyright © 2012 by Allison Lee Johnson

All rights reserved. Except for use in any review, the reproduction or utilization of this work in whole or in part in any form by any electronic, mechanical or other means, now known or hereafter invented, including xerography, photocopying and recording, or in any information storage or retrieval system, is forbidden without the written permission of the publisher, Harlequin Enterprises Limited, 225 Duncan Mill Road, Don Mills, Ontario M3B 3K9, Canada.

This is a work of fiction. Names, characters, places and incidents are either the product of the author's imagination or are used fictitiously, and any resemblance to actual persons, living or dead, business establishments, events or locales is entirely coincidental.

This edition published by arrangement with Harlequin Books S.A.

For questions and comments about the quality of this book please contact us at Customer_eCare@Harlequin.ca.

® and TM are trademarks of Harlequin Books S.A., used under license. Trademarks indicated with ® are registered in the United States Patent and Trademark Office, the Canadian Trade Marks Office and in other countries.

www.Harlequin.com

Printed in U.S.A.

Books by Allison Leigh

Harlequin Special Edition

§*The Rancher's Dance* #2110
§*Courtney's Baby Plan* #2132
§*A Weaver Proposal* #2174

Silhouette Special Edition

†*Stay...* #1170
†*The Rancher and the Redhead* #1212
†*A Wedding for Maggie* #1241
†*A Child for Christmas* #1290
Millionaire's Instant Baby #1312
†*Married to a Stranger* #1336
Mother in a Moment #1367
Her Unforgettable Fiancé #1381
The Princess and the Duke #1465
Montana Lawman #1497
Hard Choices #1561
Secretly Married #1591
Home on the Ranch #1633
The Truth About the Tycoon #1651
All He Ever Wanted #1664
The Tycoon's Marriage Bid #1707
A Montana Homecoming #1718
‡*Mergers & Matrimony* #1761
Just Friends? #1810
†*Sarah and the Sheriff* #1819
†*Wed in Wyoming* #1833
***A Cowboy Under Her Tree* #1869
††*The Bride and the Bargain* #1882
**The Boss's Christmas Proposal* #194
§*Valentine's Fortune* #1951
†*A Weaver Wedding* #1965
†*A Weaver Baby* #2000
†*A Weaver Holiday Homecoming* #201
‡‡*The Billionaire's Baby Plan* #2048
††*Once Upon a Proposal* #2078
§§*Fortune's Proposal* #2090

†Men of the Double C Ranch
§Return to the Double C
**Montana Mavericks: Striking It Rich
‡Family Business
††The Hunt for Cinderella
*Back in Business
~The Fortunes of Texas: Return to Red Rock
§§The Fortunes of Texas: Lost...and Found
‡‡The Baby Chase

Other titles by Allison Leigh available in ebook format.

ALLISON LEIGH

There is a saying that you can never be too rich or too thin. Allison doesn't believe that, but she does believe that you can *never* have enough books! When her stories find a way into the hearts—and bookshelves—of others, Allison says she feels she's done something right. Making her home in Arizona with her husband, she enjoys hearing from her readers at Allison@allisonleigh.com or P.O. Box 40772, Mesa AZ 85274-0772.

For Greg.
Because you never fail to make me laugh.

Prologue

"Don't pay any attention to him, Syd. He's full of it."

Sydney Forrest hugged her arms around her chest. She could hear her sister's voice, but it was overridden by the loud tones of her father's still ringing inside her head.

You're a worthless slut.

Just like your mother.

She stared out the windows overlooking the long, sloping green lawns that spread from their house down to the white-steepled stables. Her dark-haired father was striding across them, his long legs eating up the distance as he headed for the only thing—as far as she could tell—that he did care about.

The Forrest's Crossing Thoroughbreds. They even came before Forco, the family's textile business. At least that's what her sister Charlotte was always saying.

Char wanted to run the huge business someday. As far as Sydney was concerned, her sister was welcome to it.

The same went for her older brother Jake—he was studying agribusiness at college. Whatever the heck that was.

"It was only a kiss," Charlotte continued from behind her. She was being as practical as ever. "No big deal."

It had been a big deal to Sydney.

She was fourteen years old, and it had been her first kiss. Her first *real* kiss.

"I wonder if he'd have cared so much if I'd been kissing the son of one of his country club friends," she said bitterly. "Instead of one of the boys from the stable."

Charlotte threw her arm around Sydney's shoulders. She pressed her head against Sydney's, her blond hair a sharp contrast to Sydney's raven-black tresses. "Who knows?" she asked on a sigh. At eighteen, she was four years older than Sydney and decades smarter. Charlotte had kissed plenty of boys, but *she* knew better than to be caught doing so anywhere around Forrest's Crossing. "Didn't help that he's obviously been drinking." She waved her hand at the crystal decanter that was sitting, unstoppered, on the desk. "If you really like Andy, just meet him in town. Or at school," she advised. "The old man never has to know."

"Am I really just like her?"

Charlotte didn't have to ask what Sydney meant. "You don't remember what she looked like when she left?"

Sydney shook her head. She wanted to think she remembered her mother. But what she remembered of the woman who'd abandoned her three children when Sydney was a baby was more likely just wishful thinking.

As wishful as thinking that her father had any affection at all for the children his wife had given him—particularly Sydney.

Charlotte crossed their father's study to his desk. She tipped the pens and pencils out of a silver mint julep cup—the only thing besides the decanter sitting on top of the gleaming wood surface—and fished the desk key out from the bottom. Opening the locked center drawer, she moved a few things, then pulled out a ragged-edged snapshot. She held it up. "Just 'cause you look like her doesn't mean you are like her," she warned.

Still feeling bruised from her father's tirade, Sydney took the photograph. Black hair. Thin face. Blue eyes. They were the same eyes that stared back at Sydney whenever she looked in a mirror.

She *was* just like her mother.

"Jake looks like the old man and he's nothing like him," Charlotte added. He really was the spitting image of their father.

"He doesn't even like any of us." Sydney crumpled the photograph in her fist. "So why'd he bother fighting to keep us?"

"To win," Charlotte answered immediately.

Sydney tossed the crumpled picture on the center of the spotless desk. She didn't care if it did mean he'd know they'd been into his desk or not. "If we had four hooves and won races would he love us?"

"Do what I do, Syd." Charlotte flicked the balled-up photo with her finger and it rolled off the desk onto the floor. "Stop caring *what* he thinks." She relocked the drawer, dropped the key in the julep cup and replaced the pens and pencils before heading for the doorway. "He's not worth it," she said before sailing out of the office.

Easy for her sister to say. She was going away to college in the fall and wouldn't even be living at home. Jake, of course, was already out on his own and had been for years.

Sydney would be stuck at home with the man for several years yet.

She turned back to look out the windows. The horse barns where her father's pride and joy was stabled were visible in the distance. "He's not worth it," she repeated.

But her chest hurt and tears crept down her cheeks when she finally looked away.

She picked up the crumpled picture of her mother and smoothed it out on the desk.

Black hair. Thin face. Blue eyes.

"You're not worth it, either," she whispered to the picture.

The large grandfather clock against the wall ticked softly.

Sydney made a face and slowly picked up the photo.

She folded it carefully in half.

Then she pushed it into her pocket and left the room.

Chapter One

"What on earth are you doing here?" Sydney murmured the question to herself as she yanked a thick sweater over her head. She was wearing two layers of sweaters, on top of a long-sleeved thermal undershirt, and she still couldn't get warm. January in Wyoming was a long way from January in Georgia.

She shook her head sharply, freeing the ends of her hair from the turtleneck and pulled the cuffs of the sweater even farther down over her hands as she gave the furnace a baleful look.

The offending item was housed behind a door—currently open—off her small kitchen. After failing to get the thing to run for the last forty-eight hours, and considering her dwindling supply of firewood, she'd finally given up and called a repair service.

That had been nearly eight hours ago.

They'd promised to send someone in two.

Clearly, the three impatient calls that she'd made since then hadn't sped things along.

Not for the first time, she wondered if moving herself—lock, stock and metaphorical barrel—out to this small town in Wyoming was a monumental mistake.

But making monumental mistakes was truly the one thing at which Sydney Forrest excelled.

She rubbed her hands down her flat belly, then picked up the hammer she'd been trying not to pitch at the broken furnace and eyed the cabin wall again. She'd already hung one of her Solieres and had two more to go.

The modern American style of the paintings didn't match the cabin's interior—early-American leftover—but she loved the original oils, anyway. They were the first pieces of art she'd ever purchased, and the only ones in her sizeable collection that she'd bothered bringing with her to Weaver, Wyoming. The rest she'd left back in Georgia on loan to various galleries and she could honestly say she didn't care whether she ever saw any of them again.

But the Solieres…these, she loved.

If she could hang them here, then she'd be home.

She hoped.

She placed the nail and hammered it into the thick log wall. Only when she stopped did she realize that someone was hammering at her door, too.

She dropped the hammer on the hideous green-and-orange-plaid couch that came with the place and headed toward the door, only to stop short.

She eyed the thick, glossy-covered book lying on her couch. *The Next Forty Weeks.* Maybe it was silly of her, but she shoved it behind a cushion, anyway, before hurrying the few steps to the door.

"You're late," she said flatly when she threw open the door.

The tall man standing on the doorstep of the cabin tilted down the dark glasses he was wearing and looked at her over the rims. "I am?"

The fact that there was amusement in the bright green eyes he trained on her face didn't help her irritation. "I called for you nearly eight hours ago." Her voice was only a few shades warmer than the cold air that seeped inside around him. "I don't know what kind of service your employer expects you to provide but he assured me—more than once over those hours—that you would be...*right* here." She sounded like a witch and didn't particularly care. She pointed her index finger at the offending furnace. "It's over there."

Still peering over the tops of his sunglasses, he finally shifted away in the direction she was pointing. "I see." He stepped past her into the cabin, turning slightly sideways as he did so.

To avoid touching her, or to even fit through the door, she wasn't sure. He was wearing a thick down jacket that, despite the rip in one shoulder seam, nevertheless made his shoulders look a good six inches wider than they probably were.

"Let's just take a look, then," he murmured as he passed her.

She shivered and slammed the door shut.

She wasn't going to remotely entertain the idea that she was reacting to his deep, soft voice.

She was absolutely done with men.

Been there. Done that. With far too many.

She folded her arms around her waist and watched him as he crouched down in front of the furnace. His thighs strained against the faded, dirty jeans he was wearing and she wasn't going to admit that she, even for one moment, glanced at his rear visible beneath the coat he wasn't bothering to remove.

Why would he take it off?

The cabin's interior was freezing.

Her irritation mounted even more. "Didn't you even bring a *tool*box? What kind of a repairman are you, besides a late one?"

He glanced at her over his shoulder. He'd pulled off his sunglasses and she got a full-on view of that scruffy face and striking eyes.

He needed a shave, a haircut and, she was betting, a shower.

"Actually, I have a toolbox in my truck." His drawl seemed to have deepened. "Ma'am," he added after a moment.

Her lips tightened.

Smart-aleck repairmen she didn't need. What she *did* need was heat. Or she was afraid she was going to have to give up the idea of staying in the cabin on her own.

She might as well have a tail that she could tuck between her legs if she had to admit, already, that she couldn't hack it by herself in Weaver.

The idea tasted bitter. As bitter as the fear that ran deep and strong inside her that she *wouldn't* be able to hack it.

And then where would she be?

Back in Georgia? Lolling away her time and inheritance in a place where nobody really cared about her—or heaven forbid—felt sorry for her?

No, thanks.

"If you wouldn't mind getting to it, then," she prompted flatly when the guy just kept watching her. She was used to men watching her, but seriously, he wasn't at all her type. She didn't go for unshaven, unkempt laborers even if he did come with a pair of emerald eyes. For all she knew he had a wife and a half-dozen kids waiting for him back at his single-wide trailer.

But even her judgmental thoughts shamed her. She hugged her arms around her waist.

Weaver was supposed to be a chance for her new life.

A better life.

That was the whole point of this. A better life.

More importantly a better *Sydney* now that it wasn't only herself she had to think about.

This man, emerald eyes and all, was entirely incidental.

She cleared her throat and made herself walk a few steps closer. "I'm not used to this type of furnace," she admitted. Back home, the climate controls were the very best that money could buy. If she had to push a button, that was doing a lot. "I know it runs on gas and I already had that checked. Yesterday. The guy from the gas company said there weren't any leaks."

"Yesterday." His eyebrows—several shades darker than his blondish-brown hair—shot up a little. "You haven't had heat since then? You know it's barely thirty degrees out there. Why didn't you call before now?"

"I do know. And I did." Her voice was bordering on withering and she tried not to cringe. "I found a listing for handyman services and called this morning," she added, determined to sound friendlier. The guy was here. Finally. She needed him to fix the darn thing, not leave because she was acting like a witch.

He looked back at the furnace and shook his head. "Warned Jake that furnace was on its last legs."

She frowned a little at his easy mention of her brother, but told herself that was all probably part and parcel of living in a small town.

Everyone knew everyone.

The repairman shifted and leaned down closer to the furnace. "At least you had the sense to check for a gas leak."

It didn't sound like praise to her. "I'm not an idiot." Not about everything, at least.

He gave her a glance again with that amused glint in his eyes that put her teeth on edge. "Didn't say otherwise. Ma'am," he said mildly. Then he pulled off a panel and set it on the floor beside him, studying the inside of the furnace for a moment before reaching in and fiddling with something, then pushing to his feet. He turned to her. "I'll be back."

He walked past her and went out the door, closing it behind him.

She shivered again and stared at the guts of the furnace, visible behind the missing panel. It might as well have been a nuclear reactor for all of the sense it made to her.

Through the wide window next to the door she could see him stomping across the snowy ground to a big pickup truck. It was so filthy she couldn't even tell what color it was, unless *mud* had a place now on the spectrum. He pulled open the door and climbed up inside.

Then he just sat there with the door open, despite how cold she knew it was outside, his sunglasses back in place while he looked at the cabin.

Even from her distance she could see him shake his head.

Her lips tightened again.

She deliberately turned away and picked up the large, square painting and fit it over the sturdy nail, nudging up one corner until she was satisfied. Then she stepped back to survey her work.

But even her satisfaction at having her favorite paintings hanging in her new home didn't help her forget the man in his truck outside.

She could practically feel his gaze burning through the window.

She picked up her hammer again and set the next nail where she'd already measured off the spot and in just a few minutes, she had the third and last painting hanging in place.

She looked out the window again. Now the man—still sitting in his truck—was talking on a cell phone.

She exhaled noisily and went into the kitchen. It didn't possess a microwave. Nor a dishwasher. And the pot filled with water that she put on the stove was hardly the latest in design when it came to making coffee.

But then coffee wasn't on her list of allowable drinks any longer.

She turned on the flame beneath the pot and emptied a packet of hot chocolate mix into a thick, white mug. If her furnace wasn't working by that evening, she might have to go stay at her brother's new house.

It was what he'd wanted her to do in the first place. The cabin was barely habitable, he'd said. Sydney figured what he really meant was that it would be barely habitable for *her,* given her usual taste for luxury with a capital *L*. He and his wife had left for California the day after she'd arrived four days ago, taking their aunt and her new husband with them. They'd already planned to spend a month visiting Jake's twin sons, who spent part of the year there with their mother. But no. Sydney had insisted that she was determined to do this on her own. That she loved the quaint little place where she could have all the privacy that she desired.

Jake had just shrugged and told her she'd always been stubborn about getting her own way. What he hadn't added, but had probably thought was, *even when it was a mistake.*

Mistake or not, she'd set a course, and she was determined to stick to it. Her brother didn't know the entire reason she'd sought refuge in Weaver. She'd tell him when she was ready. But right now, she couldn't bear to admit failure already, and that's how it felt if she had to give up and go stay at his place.

A failure.

She leaned against the knotty pine cupboards that formed the small L-shaped kitchen and waited for the water to heat. Small bubbles were just beginning to form in the base of the pot when she heard the door open again and she peered around the short wall into the main room of the cabin.

The sunglasses were gone. But the repairman still wasn't carrying any tools.

"How long do you think this is going to take?"

"Not long." He crossed to the closet and crouched down. "My tool." He removed a long-nosed lighter from inside his coat, giving her that amused look again. "Pilot light is out. And you need the light to have heat." He leaned down again toward the furnace, his broad body blocking her view.

She could feel her nerves tightening up all over again in the face of his exaggerated patience. "Wait," she said sharply.

He hesitated and glanced back. "Thought you were in a hurry for some heat. Ma'am."

She really detested his way of tacking that last bit on, as if by reluctant duty, and she gave him an icy look. "I want to see what you're doing."

He just shrugged as if he didn't care one way or the other, and he waited until she turned off the stove and forced herself to crouch down beside him. The smell of him hit her just as strongly as she'd feared.

Just not in the way she'd feared.

Because he didn't smell as dirty as he looked. He smelled fresh. Like the first scent of the wide outdoors that she'd gotten when she'd climbed out of her car after driving hours and hours and hours from Georgia to Weaver. Vaguely pine-like. Vaguely earthy. Fresh. Breathtaking.

She realized his gaze was slanting over her and blamed her crazy hormones when she felt her face actually start to warm. She'd stopped blushing when she was about ten years old. It had to be her hormones that were causing her to think this man smelled enticing. Same way her hormones had told her she absolutely had to have both sliced pickles and potato chips on the peanut butter sandwich she'd eaten for breakfast. "*Well?* Are you going to show me or not?"

His eyebrows lifted a little and his jaw canted slightly to one side as he gave his head the faintest of shakes. But regardless of his personal opinion—obviously lacking—where she was concerned, he tapped one long index finger against a knob. "This controls whether the pilot is on or off. I turned it off before I went outside." He turned it, and a bit of dried blood on his scratched knuckle stood out. "Turn it to where it says Pilot." He held up the long lighter with his other hand and clicked it on. A small flame burst from the end and he tucked it inside the furnace, angling his messy head a little in front of her so he could see.

He really did have thick hair.

She averted her eyes back to what he was doing.

"Set the flame there," he continued, "and keep the knob pushed down." He pulled out the lighter, letting the flame die.

But she could see the small blue flame burning inside the furnace and ferociously kept her gaze on it, even though she could feel him looking at her again. Then he abruptly leaned down and blew out the tiny flame.

"Here." He held out the lighter. "You wanted to learn, right?"

She nodded and took the lighter, careful not to touch his greasy fingers.

His lips twisted, as if he noticed. But all he said was, "Don't be afraid. You'll never know unless you try."

She hesitantly pressed the knob where he indicated, clicked the lighter and set the flame where he had.

"That's it. Give it about a minute, then let up on the knob." She did as he said and he showed her that the pilot remained lit. "Thermocouple sensed the flame, which triggered the gas valve, and hello, heat. Turn the knob from Pilot to On…you see?" He waited until she nodded and then he put the panel back in place. "You oughta be good to go."

He pushed to his feet, walked to the other side of the room and held his hand over the register for a moment. "It's coming." His gaze passed from her face to her newly hung paintings then back to her again.

She'd straightened, too. There was no question that he didn't appreciate her modern artwork. It was as plain on his face as his amusement, and her temper glowed warm all over again. "I assume your employer will send a bill." It wasn't a question. "I'd have given you a tip if I hadn't had to wait eight hours for you to show up."

Derek Clay managed to keep from grinning outright as he looked at Sydney Forrest, the sister of his cousin's husband.

He'd come by the place to check on her as a courtesy, since he lived closest to the out-of-the-way cabin that she'd moved herself and her ugly paintings into a few days ago. And while he was genuinely concerned that she'd been living without heat, he wasn't all that interested in the woman herself.

Definitely a looker. But he knew from Jake that she liked living in the fast lane. Along with that, she was snooty. And undoubtedly high-maintenance coming from the moneyed background that she had. None of these qualities was high on his list of attractive attributes in a woman, no matter *how* good she looked.

"I'm sure they'll appreciate the prompt payment," he offered, then stuck out his hand. "I'm Derek, by the way."

She eyed his hand—which admittedly had a smear of grease on the back of it and had since he'd been wrangling with an ancient tractor engine inside which his mom's latest cat had decided to have her kittens—with clear distaste. But then she seemed to swallow hard and stuck her slender hand briefly into his. "Sydney Forrest," she offered.

"I know. You're Jake's sis."

Her fine, dark eyebrows drew together over a narrow nose that tilted up just a bit at the end, saving her oval face from being too classically pretty. "*You* know my brother?"

Her tone implied that anyone of his ilk couldn't possibly, and despite his efforts, his ornery grin cracked through. "'Fraid so, Syd." He couldn't help laying on the hick, given her obviously appalled reaction. "You and me? We're practically kin seein' how your brother's hitched to my cousin."

He didn't think her ivory face could get any whiter, but it did. "You're…related to J.D.?" Her rosy lips spread in a thin smile that wasn't reflected at all in her dark blue eyes.

"Yup. Derek Clay. So some might even call you and

me *kissin'* cousins," he added, because she obviously was not going to see the humor in any of this.

Still, something about the situation left him feeling itchy and irritated because—snooty or not—she *was* pretty damn beautiful.

Her eyes were a deep, dark blue and now, as a steely glint came into them, they iced over. They reminded him of black ice.

"You could have just told me who you were." Her voice was cold as a witch's behind, but the cadence of her words nevertheless had an almost hypnotic molasses-smooth sway.

"You maybe could have waited three seconds for me to do so before jumping on that high horse of assumptions you ride," he returned blandly. "Don't worry your pretty head any, though. I won't tell if you won't."

"You can tell whomever you like." Her vaguely pointy chin was set. "*I've* done nothing wrong."

"No, ma'am," Derek agreed. She was no more in the right or wrong than he was, when it came down to it. Still, her snooty attitude wouldn't get her anywhere in Weaver, even though she *was* Jake's sister and thereby connected to the Clay family, which was generally well thought of in the community. "I guess you haven't."

And since she was connected to the Clays—to him—he pushed aside his general irritation with himself *and* her and reminded himself of the way he was raised.

He looked past her sweater-bundled shoulder into the cabin's interior. "Watch that pilot light," he warned. "If the thermocouple is failing, it'll go out again no matter how careful you are. And don't wait an entire day to ask for help when you need it."

She crossed her arms and managed to look down her narrow, turned-up, sexy nose at him, even though she stood about a head shorter than his six-three. "I did call for help," she reminded him as if he were dense enough to have somehow missed that point.

"Did you call the number for the Double-C that Jake left you?" He didn't need to see the chagrin she tried to hide to know that she hadn't. He'd been at the Double-C since before dawn that day working with his father, Matthew Clay, who ran the family ranch. If Jake's sister had called, he'd have known about it.

She hadn't called.

"I didn't want to impose." Now that enticing sway to her voice had gone all stiff.

And he was irritated all over again with himself because he felt some regret for that. "Nobody in the Clay family would consider it an imposition. Maybe you'd know that if you'd have bothered to come to Jake and J.D.'s wedding last summer and taken time to get to know us."

Her jaw dropped a little. "Is that what *Jake* said? Or is this just your know-it-all take on it?"

Jake hadn't said a word against his sister. "Weddings tend to bring out the crowds in my family."

"As they do in mine," she returned coolly. "If I could have made it, I would have. I was here for my Aunt Susan's wedding to Stan Ventura a few months ago. He's sort of family to you Clays now, isn't he, yet I don't recall seeing *you* there."

He had missed that wedding, but not because he'd wanted to. "I was in Cheyenne. On business." He gave the lie with no regret. He'd been attending a funeral.

She smiled with no humor. "Is that an excuse that only applies to you? Maybe I was away on business when Jake and J.D. were married."

"Were you?"

Her head tilted slightly and her shining blue-black hair slid away from her high, patrician cheekbone. “Yes.”

“And what *is* your business, Sydney Forrest? I hadn’t heard that you worked for Forco.”

Her chin rose a little. “My sister and brother run Forco. I sit on the board.”

“Anything else?”

“Racehorses and art.”

In her Southern warm-honey voice, *art* came out more like *ahhht,* and it sent heat down his spine that he didn’t welcome. “Art like those monstrosities you hung on the wall in there?” He jerked his chin over her shoulder.

“I suppose you prefer a paint-by-the-numbers nude lounging on black velvet?”

“Don’t go knocking the combination of velvet and naked skin until you’ve tried it.” He leaned closer. “Kissin’ cousin.”

She jerked back, a flash coming and going in her eyes. “I cannot believe you are even related to J.D. She is perfectly lovely and you are—”

“—not a woman, that’s for sure.”

“Odious,” she finished, witheringly.

“And you’re a snob,” he countered. “You work on that little problem, cupcake, and I’ll work on mine.”

“Cupcake?” Her eyes narrowed to slits and she took a step back, shutting the door smack in his face.

Not that he didn’t deserve it.

If he had a door to slam in her face, he’d probably do it, too.

“Nice meeting you, cuz,” he said loudly through the door. Then he turned away and headed toward his truck.

He’d give her about a week, and then she’d be hightailing it back to her pampered life in Georgia.

As far as he'd ever been able to tell, that's what spoiled rich girls always did when the going got tough. Ran.

He reached the truck and swung up into the driver's seat, looking back at the cabin despite his intention not to.

She was looking back at him.

Hard to tell which one of them looked away first.

Derek's pride hoped it wasn't him. But with the tires crunching over the snow as he turned a wide circle, he had to admit that it might well have been.

Chapter Two

Sydney had come to Weaver for lots of reasons. Some were more immediate than others, but none of them were unimportant. Rebuilding a relationship with her brother was one. Or—she thought with brutal honesty—*establishing* a relationship with her brother was a better way to put it since—aside from the occasional racehorse she found for Forrest's Crossing, which Jake still ran even though he'd moved to Wyoming—they'd had little to do with one another for years.

And yes, she *had* missed his wedding to J. D. Clay. She still felt guilty about it, because she could have made it if she'd really tried. But she truly hadn't believed that he would care much one way or another, and despite her Aunt Susan's urging, she'd pulled her usual Sydney act. She'd commissioned a crystal statuette of Latitude—a Thoroughbred her brother was particularly fond of—and had it delivered to him and J.D. before the wedding.

But she hadn't left Antoine's side where they'd been staying in Antibes at the home of a particularly discriminating art collector. Mostly because she was well aware that Antoine was taking his newest assistant with him on the trip, and said assistant was ten years younger than Sydney, particularly pretty and clearly looking to be *more* than an assistant.

Despite Sydney's absence from the nuptials, J.D. had called her, thanking her for the incredibly beautiful gift. Sydney wasn't surprised by that. She'd met J.D. on a few occasions when she'd been working for Jake at Forrest's Crossing. The other woman had always been professionally courteous. But after J.D.'s call had come Jake's, and he'd been rather less courteous when he'd told Sydney that J.D. assumed Sydney didn't approve of their marriage.

It couldn't have been further from the truth.

Which was why Sydney was now picking her way through the snow behind her cabin to the shed that acted as a garage and storage for a bunch of tractor-size tools.

Maggie Clay—J.D.'s mother and yet another one of the seemingly endless Clays that Weaver possessed—had called her the evening before to insist that she join the family for dinner out at the family's ranch. "Sunday" dinner, which Sydney knew from her brother was usually a family affair. Since Sydney had some bridges to build, she knew she might as well start doing it now, even if J.D. and Jake *were* in California.

And if nothing else, the place where the meal was being held—the Double-C—was bound to be warm, which was more than could be said of her cabin right now, since the furnace had quit on her again this morning.

So she climbed into her little red convertible two-seater and prayed the engine would start.

The import was nearly thirty years old and had belonged to her mother. A gift from Sydney's father, until he'd taken it back from her during the divorce. He'd later given it to Sydney as a gift—not because he was bestowing some treasured thing upon her—but because it was a manual transmission. After she'd backed one of Forrest's Crossing's trucks through a paddock fence, he'd mockingly laughed that, like her mother, she'd never be able to drive it properly, anyway.

"Just a little paternal adoration," she murmured now as she coaxed the engine to life.

Bringing the car with her here to Wyoming had probably been the height of folly. But no more, possibly, than bringing herself had been.

When it came down to it, she was about as equipped for the practical matters of life here as her red demon was equipped for snow-covered roads and frozen temperatures.

"But we'll both do it, won't we? We *have* to." She ignored the faint edge of desperation she felt and patted the steering wheel when the engine finally caught.

She wasn't quite sure what she'd have done if it hadn't started. Did Weaver even possess a cab company?

Somehow, she doubted it.

Fortunately, it hadn't snowed since she'd arrived, so the bumpy drive that led from the highway to the cabin was still clear and she made it out of the shed and down to the main road with no engine stalls. Then it was just a matter of following the instructions Maggie had given her to reach the "big house" on the family's cattle ranch.

Sydney realized soon enough that the place was no more "in Weaver" than the cabin was. When she finally pulled to a stop in front of a sprawling stone house, there were already a half-dozen cars parked in the curving drive in front of it. She pulled as close to the snow-plowed edge of the drive as she dared, parking behind an enormous black SUV, and climbed out, smoothing down her cashmere coat as she eyed the vehicles. Everything from economy cars to luxury SUVs. Jake had told her the Clays were a diverse bunch.

Even their automobiles reflected it.

She carefully picked her way between the vehicles toward the snowy ground separating the plowed drive from the house, wincing a little as her high, stacked heels sank into the snow. Her boots were suede and not meant for getting wet. She needed to shop. And soon.

"We were about ready to send out a search crew."

The low, masculine voice startled her and she jerked her head up to see Derek Clay standing on the wide porch that stretched across the front of the house. He was wearing jeans again—though this time at least they looked clean. The down coat was gone, but all that did was show off the shoulders stretching the limits of his untucked, navy blue pullover. Evidently the down coat he'd worn the day before hadn't been solely responsible for the wide shoulders.

Sydney also noted the arm he had looped possessively over the shoulder of a very pretty young woman. Whether this was another cousin of the "kissing" variety or not, Sydney could see she was considerably younger than Derek. She was guessing he was closer to Sydney's thirty-one than the girl's probable twenty-one.

Men were men, obviously. And for a good many of them, the younger their companions were, the better.

Not that she cared one whit that Derek seemed no better than Antoine had been in that regard.

She yanked the lapels of her coat more tightly around

her waist as she gingerly picked her way through the snow until she reached the shoveled walkway.

"As you can see, I made it." She even managed a smile, though how she did after their encounter the day before was a minor miracle.

"Small wonder," he returned and nodded his head toward her car. "We have snowdrifts bigger than that toy." He might have cleaned up in the clothing department, but the dark blond waves of his hair were still as unkempt as ever. "J.D. and Jake have plenty of suitable vehicles up at their place. Why not use one?"

His tone made it perfectly clear that he considered her brainless for not having done so, and Sydney's jaw ached as she locked her insincere smile in place. "I'm surprised Jake didn't tell you already. I *like* unsuitable," she assured him blithely, though nothing could have been further from the truth.

Yes, she'd frequently indulged in the unsuitable. More often than not. But that was exactly what had led her to this particular point in her life.

Nausea nudged at her, deep inside, like the low tide getting ready to come in.

She swallowed hard and took a deep breath of cold, bracing air as she crossed the walkway to the shallow steps leading up to the house.

"Unsuitable doesn't fly real well in these parts," Derek said when she reached the top. "Thinking about safety does."

His companion—who looked even more dewy and fresh up close—didn't bother trying to hide the elbow that she poked into his side. "Be nice," she said, and stuck out her hand toward Sydney. "I'm Tabby Taggart. And not all of us are quite the sticks in the mud as this guy is."

Sydney shook the girl's hand. "I'm Sydney." She wasn't

going to comment on the sticks business, even if she did happen to agree. “It’s nice to meet you, Tabby.” She let her gaze take in both of them. “I apologize for running a little late.”

“No worries.” Tabby waved an unconcerned hand and without losing Derek’s arm, pulled open the enormous front door with obvious familiarity. “When there’s a crowd around here for Sunday dinner it always takes a bit of doing to get the meal on the table, anyway. And can I just say that I love those boots of yours? I hope you’ve treated the suede for getting wet, though.”

Over the girl’s head, Sydney’s gaze ran into Derek’s and she cursed herself for being caught looking his way.

“Wouldn’t worry about the boots, Tab,” he said as they headed inside. “Sydney’s an honest-to-God heiress, remember? If she wanted to pretend they’re disposable after one wearing, she could.”

Tabby looked up at him, grabbed his face in her hand and planted a kiss on his lips. “Funny guy, aren’t you?” Then she gave his cheek a playful slap.

“Deathly,” Sydney murmured, watching the girl move off. Tabby could think her boyfriend was joking, but Sydney knew he wasn’t. She wasn’t dressed appropriately for the weather any more than her car was suited to it.

In his eyes it was obviously just one more strike against her.

She wondered what he’d think if he knew that his strikes were small potatoes in comparison to the ones she’d had leveled at her since childhood. But then again, she’d rather he didn’t know. Thinking she was a snob was much better than knowing what she really was.

A pregnant, rejected fool who’d never accomplished anything on her own.

Fortunately, her arrival had been noticed, not just by Maggie Clay, the woman who'd invited her, but by countless others who quickly surrounded her. Maggie, who was just as blonde as her daughter, J.D., grabbed Sydney's hand as if she were five and began introducing everyone even as she took Sydney's coat and thrust it at Derek with instructions to hang it up.

As Sydney struggled to keep up with the introductions—some familiar and some not—a part of her couldn't help wondering if she'd find her coat later hanging from some tree outside when he disappeared with it.

"Oh, my goodness, what a fabulous dress! Is it actually leather?" The petite brunette, whom Maggie had just introduced as Tara, was definitely not one of the individuals that Sydney recalled from Susan and Stan's wedding. The other woman barely waited for Sydney's nod before she continued gushing. "If I could get some items like that for the shop, I'd sell them out in a heartbeat no matter what price tag I put on them." She grinned ruefully as she ran her hand over the noticeably pregnant bulge stretching out the front of her cherry-red sweater. "Not that *I'm* likely to ever be able to wear anything cut so narrowly again."

Sydney could have laughed—or cried—at the irony.

"Tara owns Classic Charms down on Main Street," Maggie explained. "She has the most wonderfully eclectic collection. Everything from furniture to clothing."

Tara shrugged dismissively. "Not everything. But I do like to have some unusual items, and that dress would definitely be one. Vintage?"

Again, Sydney nodded. She glanced down at the caramel-colored leather dress that draped from her shoulders to just above her knees. "I found it in a secondhand shop in Paris a few years ago." She loved it and was determined to wear it as long as she could. "But I can see that I *am* overdressed," she admitted. Nearly everyone there was dressed in jeans and sweaters.

"You think?" A deep voice murmured from behind her and she didn't have to look back to know it was Derek. She'd recognize his voice anywhere now.

She ignored him and looked at Maggie beside her. "I think I should have taken notes with the introductions," she admitted. "I'm not sure I'll keep everyone straight."

Maggie laughed and squeezed Sydney's hand. "Unless you've been born into the group, we've all thought the same thing at one time or another. We're an overwhelming bunch. But you'll get used to it."

"If she's here long enough," Derek added. His tone didn't imply it, but Sydney didn't have to guess very hard to know that he was hoping she wouldn't be.

"Actually, I plan to be here a long, long while." Smiling a confident smile she didn't feel at all, she directed her comment toward the friendly Maggie.

"I know how much Jake and J.D. are hoping so," the older woman returned comfortably.

"How's that furnace holding out?"

"Just fine," she lied, finally looking Derek's way. Instead of the nubile Tabby under his arm, he was now holding a wildly giggling dark-haired imp upside down.

Her stomach took a dangerous dive and she quickly looked away. She wasn't sure if it was the baby-related nausea or the sight of that odious man looking so perfectly natural jiggling around an obviously delighted toddler.

"Derek told us you had a little problem with it." Maggie drew Sydney farther along the scarred wood floors. "He's a whiz at fixing everything. Always helps out when he's able. He's wonderful that way."

Sydney managed not to choke.

They'd reached a long dining room that was dominated by the china-and-crystal-laden table that took center stage. Three-fourths of the chairs around it were being claimed by the people who had already greeted Sydney, and Maggie led her to two on the side near the head of the table. "Come and sit here beside me. You can tell me how you're settling in at J.D. and Jake's cabin." She pulled out one chair and took the other.

"It's going fine. I'm just not sure what I'm going to do with myself now that I've finished unpacking," she admitted a little ruefully. She sat where directed and waved off the wine that Maggie offered in favor of water and turned to smile at the blond-haired teenage boy sitting on her other side, who was not very discreetly throwing wadded bits of his paper napkin at the girl sitting directly across from him.

He dropped his hands guiltily to his lap, though, when Sydney sat and almost did a double take as he gave her a lopsided grin. "Hey. I'm Eli."

"Yeah, Eli. Stop drooling over the lady and move it. You're in my seat," Derek said behind them. He set a long-necked bottle of beer next to the empty wine glass near his plate and jerked his thumb.

Sydney's stomach sank as the lanky boy slid out of the chair and moved to the other side of the table. "Nobody wants to sit next to their sister," he complained, giving the target of his napkin wads a little shove before slouching into the chair next to her.

"Nearly everyone at this table is a sister or brother of someone," Maggie said without heat.

"And if not that, then cousins," Derek added as he took the vacated seat.

Sydney ignored him. She noticed that Tabby was sitting on the other side of the table, several seats down from Derek, between Tara on one side and a toffee-haired young man on the other. Maggie had mentioned his name. Jared. Justin. Something like that. But he was Maggie's nephew, that she was certain of. And the young man was graced with the unfair quantity of "wow" genes that all of the Clays seemed to possess.

Maggie was nodding toward the empty seats at the end of the table. "It's too bad that Gloria and Squire are gone right now." Her hand had come to rest over the bronzed hand of her husband, sitting on her other side and now, she patted it. "Daniel's father. I know you met at your aunt's wedding. I'm sure they're looking forward to seeing you again."

They hadn't had time to speak much at the wedding since Sydney had only been there for a matter of hours, but she did remember the iron-haired man who was the patriarch of this large, rambunctious family and his wife. "Jake mentioned they were away for a few weeks?"

"Yeah, Squire doesn't like the cold winters so much anymore," added another man as he entered and took the chair at the head of the table. He was blond as well, though with plenty of silver shot through the brutally short, thick strands, and his eyes were the palest blue she'd ever seen. For someone old enough to be her father, he, too, was ridiculously handsome.

"I'm Matthew," he said. "Welcome to the Double-C."

"Daniel's brother," Maggie provided from her side.

"My father," Derek added from her other.

Sydney's gaze flicked back to the older man. It irritated the life out of her when she realized she was looking for some resemblance between him and his son. Aside from the fair hair—which on Derek was a whole lot darker than his father—the likeness was slim. Despite the dark stubble liberally shadowing Derek's jaw, she figured his face was less squarely, ruggedly male than his father's.

No less good-looking, whether she wanted to admit that or not, but in a prettier way.

Then, she couldn't help a small smile. She didn't know much about Derek Clay, but she couldn't help but figure he wouldn't appreciate being called *pretty.* "Thank you," she told Matthew, glad that her private amusement at Derek's expense would simply be taken at face value. "Your ranch is quite something to see."

"Oh, darling, you have barely scratched the surface." Jaimie—the auburn-haired woman who'd obviously passed on her finer features to her son Derek—angled between their chairs to set an enormous platter in the center of the table. She swatted Derek's hand when he reached out to grab one of the pizza boxes that were incongruously stacked high on the china platter. "Wait until after grace," she chided.

Sydney sent him a sideways look as his mother moved away to take her place adjacent to her husband's. But instead of looking cowed by his mother, he was just eyeing Sydney with that vaguely challenging, amused look. She was beginning to wonder if he had it all the time, or if he'd reserved it just for her.

But then, when Maggie clasped her hand and she noticed that everyone around the table was doing the same, she realized what "grace" meant to these people.

She reluctantly set her palm into the upturned one that Derek had rested on the table between their two plates and it took all of her willpower not to jerk it back when his long fingers closed over hers, capturing it but good.

He, she noted, didn't close his eyes or bow his head even a fraction, as his father gave a brief blessing for the meal.

And when the amen was said and everyone turned their attention to the meal, and pizza boxes were thrown open and passed hither and yon, Sydney spread her napkin on her lap and eyed him. "Not showing a lot of reverence there, were you?" She kept her voice low, even though she doubted her words would be carried beyond his ears, since everyone's mouths—if they weren't already occupied with eating—were running a mile a minute. She couldn't even begin to unravel the half-dozen conversations that seemed to be running concurrently.

"Neither were you," he countered. A few lines radiated from the corners of the green eyes that he'd clearly inherited from his mother. "Or you wouldn't have noticed what I was doing."

The fact that he was right didn't comfort her any. She managed not to snatch the pizza box he was holding aloft for her as she passed it smoothly to Maggie on her other side.

"Pizza too common-folk for you?" He jerked his chin at her empty plate.

"Not at all," she returned truthfully. She loved the stuff. But the smell of the pepperoni was luring the threatening tide inside her as surely as the moon lured the ocean. Instead, she reached for the enormous salad bowl that was sitting almost directly in front of her, and put some on her plate.

Even that, though, wasn't exactly nirvana for her senses, because there was a plentiful amount of chopped black olives among the lettuce and tomatoes.

She'd always liked black olives.

But right now, they looked as appetizing as an infestation of little black bugs.

Her fork dropped on the plate with a clatter as she hurriedly grabbed her filled water glass and, with an appalling lack of dignity, chugged half of its contents before she set it down.

Derek was watching her, the corners of his lips turned down. "What do you do? Maintain a rabbit's diet just so you can fit into look-at-me dresses like that?" His gaze dropped from her face to the dress in question and she was certain it was only irritation that made her skin beneath the garment feel hot.

"Stop teasing," Jaimie said from down the table. She was pinching off pieces of her pizza crust and setting them in front of the fat-cheeked baby occupying a high chair next to her. "As I was starting to say before, Sydney's hardly seen a fraction of the Double-C. Derek, you ought to show her around after dinner."

"Tramping through snow and cow piles with those boots of hers?" Derek shook his head as he reached out a long arm and grabbed a slice of plain cheese pizza from another box. "Probably not a good idea." He plopped the slice on Sydney's plate and pointedly moved the box as if he feared she'd be rude enough to put the slice back.

"Don't be silly." Jaimie's face was wreathed in a smile. If she recognized her son's obvious reluctance, she was ignoring it. "You can borrow something more suitable," she told Sydney. "It's worth the trouble," she promised. "Even covered in snow, the Double-C is impressive."

Sydney knew that Jake had been impressed, which was no mean feat. "I'm sure it is," she said. "But I don't want to put anyone out."

"Face it, Mom," Derek said with just enough dry humor not to sound as odious as Sydney knew he really was. "She was raised at Forrest's Crossing. She might not be that interested in our little cow operation here considering she grew up around prize-winning Thoroughbreds."

Her jaw was tightening again. She was well aware that

there was nothing "little" about the Double-C. It was the largest cattle operation in the state. She also could feel the look that Matthew was sending their way and knew, without question, that he at least was picking up on something between them.

Jake would never forgive her if she managed to alienate a single one of his beloved J.D.'s family.

She forced a smile toward Derek. "But I *am* interested," she assured him brightly. "I just don't want to be an imposition."

She hoped to heaven she was the only one who heard the faint snort he gave.

"Don't be silly," Jaimie said again. "You're family now, darling. Don't ever forget that."

"Cousins, remember?" Derek was smiling, too, though it looked a little thin around the edges as far as Sydney could tell.

"Right." She didn't even realize she'd picked up the slice of pizza until it was in her fingers and the aroma—thankfully tantalizing this time—reached her. She bit off the narrow point of the slice and nearly closed her eyes with glee as the chewy, cheesy mess practically melted on her tongue.

She heard Derek make a strangled sound and looked his way. "Are you all right?"

"Peachy." He dumped a load of salad on his own plate, jabbed his fork viciously into a tomato slice and shoved it into his mouth.

She glanced down the table toward Tabby. The girl was laughing and looking particularly animated as she talked with the good-looking young guy sitting next to her. "You have competition," she murmured to Derek. "Is that what's making you crankier than usual?"

He gave her a strange look. "What the hell are you going on about?"

She nodded toward Tabby. "Not that it's any business of mine, but he seems more suited to her. Age-wise, that is."

"You think Tabby and I are—"

"*Aren't* you?"

The corner of his lips jerked a little, then settled into a curl. "I've known her since she was in diapers."

Sydney gave him a derisive look. "Is that supposed to excuse robbing the cradle?"

He gave a bark of laughter. "Tab is Evan's little sister. Evan's married to my cousin, Leandra. They're not here today." He jabbed his fork in the direction of his mother and the high chair–corralled baby beside her. "But that's their youngest kid, Katie. And Justin—" his fork air-jabbed the young man next to Tabby "—and Tabby have been friends since their sandbox days."

Then he lowered his fork and ran his gaze over her in a way that had her nerve endings heating up all over again. "Trust me, cupcake." His voice dropped a notch. "I like my women *all* grown-up."

The pizza she'd swallowed seemed suddenly stuck like a lump in her throat. It took every inch of effort she possessed to smile casually. "I guess I misunderstood."

His eyebrow peaked, making him look devilish. "You think?"

She grabbed her water glass and downed the remainder of its contents. "I'm not going to apologize again," she said under her breath. "You deliberately misled me yesterday. And you've been needling me since."

"In case you haven't noticed, you're carrying around a pincushion of needles of your own, though God knows where you have the room in that dress you're wearing."

He looked over at his mother when she called his name and asked him to bring in the rest of the pizza.

Startled, Sydney looked over the long tabletop. “There’s more?”

Maggie laughed outright. “There’s *always* more, Sydney. One thing this family has learned how to do right together is eat.” Then she asked, “Tara, do you still need me to help out at the shop tomorrow?”

Sydney tried not to pay too much notice as Derek left the table, but it was hard considering his arm brushed against hers as he did so. She was positive he’d done it deliberately.

“If it’s not too much trouble,” Tara was saying. “I’m afraid I’m going to have to hire more help whether I want to or not.”

“You have that much business?” The second the question left her lips, Sydney realized how it might sound.

But Tara was just smiling ruefully. “Surprising, I know. But Weaver draws more people than you would think just from driving down our little old Main Street. I’m open seven days a week now, and—”

“And it’s too damn many hours,” her husband, Axel, said flatly. He was holding a squirming little boy who was clearly anxious to get down from his daddy’s lap.

“So speaks the King.” Tara held out her hands. “Give me Aidan.” Her husband immediately handed over the tot.

“Well, darling,” Jaimie inserted, “you *are* pregnant again. And getting more so by the day.”

Derek had returned and dumped three more enormous pizza boxes on top of the empties. Sydney watched with some amazement as eager hands reached out and threw them open, passing the food all over again.

"Thought you already ran an advertisement for some help," Jaimie said.

Tara shrugged. "I did a few months ago. No takers, though."

"Hire Sydney," Derek said, sitting down once more beside her. "She was just telling Mom she needed something to fill her time."

Sydney's jaw loosened a little.

He gave a little frown that she didn't buy for a second. "But then working in a local shop might be too tame for you, with your love of *racehorses and ahhht.*"

Chapter Three

He was watching her with those goading, green eyes.

"Not at all. I'd love to help." The words came out of Sydney's mouth before she could even form the thoughts.

She loved the surprised look on his face.

But when she looked beyond him, she could also see the shocked looks on the faces around her.

She had to admit that her encounter with Derek might have given him some reason to think she was a snob, but she didn't think she'd given anyone else reason to think it. And if they weren't thinking she was a snob, then they were thinking she was incapable.

She didn't *think* she was a snob. She knew she'd been afforded luxuries and opportunities that many weren't. She couldn't change the wealthy parents she'd been born to, no matter how many times she'd wished otherwise.

But *incapable?*

That was a thornier issue altogether.

She focused on Tara, who was watching her with a puzzled expression. “I *do* have oodles of time on my hands.” For now, anyway. “And though I’m sure I’m not the most qualified—” she ignored Derek’s sudden cough beside her “—I’m willing to help out until you can find a person you’d prefer more.”

“Prefer!” Tara nearly sputtered the word. “Are you kidding me? You would be perfect!”

Now it was time for Sydney to return the shocked stare.

“J.D. has told me dozens of times how impeccable your style is,” Tara was going on. “I can’t wait to pick your brain.”

Sydney wasn’t sure what was more bemusing: J.D. thinking her style was impeccable, or that Tara was actually enthusiastic about having Sydney’s help. Feeling woefully self-conscious, she laughed a little. “I’m not sure what you’ll find, but you’re welcome to pick away. You could do that even without me volunteering to help at the shop.”

Tara waved her hand. “No volunteering. I’ll hire you if you want the job. Four days a week, to start, and the money’ll—”

Sydney absolutely didn’t want to talk money in front of all these people. Derek, most of all. “We can work that out later,” she said hurriedly.

“Great. Can you start tomorrow?”

Tara’s enthusiasm was hard to resist. “Sure.” Then Sydney quickly looked toward Maggie. “Unless I’m stepping on your toes.”

“Good grief, no,” Maggie assured her. “I’ll be able to drive down and see Early and Sofia for a few hours after all. My grandchildren,” she added. “Our other daughter, Angeline, and her husband, Brody, live in Sheridan.”

"And so does Maggie half the time," Daniel drawled beside her.

She gave him a light swat. "I don't hear you complaining about it," she returned, laughing. "You're worse than I am when it comes to spending time with the grandchildren. I figured getting down there a few times a month was doing good, but you want to go at least once a week."

"All of Squire's sons take after him," Jaimie told Sydney. "But I think he's still the worst when it comes to spoiling his great-grandchildren."

"And meddling in the rest of our lives," Matthew added, looking wry. "Damned old coot."

Just listening to them made Sydney feel a little breathless. It was so plain how easily they spread their affection among each other.

There'd been family dinners among the Forrests.

But never one like this.

Her gaze ran over the jumble of informal pizza boxes and paper napkins accompanied by fine china and Waterford glassware. But it wasn't even that eclectic mix of formal and incredibly informal that was so appealing to her. It was the easy acceptance of everyone who sat around that table. From squirming toddlers to squabbling teenagers to parents and grandparents. Everyone seemed to have a say and nobody was disregarded.

"Something wrong?" Derek was holding his longneck, his thumb picking at the label. "You've got a strange look on your face."

She sat up a little straighter in her chair and folded her napkin over her empty plate. Funny. She didn't even remember eating her salad. "I can't imagine why. I was just thinking I'd never enjoyed a meal more."

His thick lashes narrowed around those brilliant eyes as he studied her. If he was looking for some hidden meaning in her words, he wasn't going to find them. "Tara's going to be counting on you now."

She folded her hands in her lap. "Your point being?"

"She doesn't deserve to be let down."

Even though she'd expected them, his words still disappointed her. And she honestly couldn't figure out why they should. Aside from his family connection to her brother, what Derek Clay thought about her or didn't think about her shouldn't matter one iota.

After all, she couldn't be a bigger disappointment to anyone than she already was to herself. But she was determined to change that; moving to Weaver had been the first step.

"You're the one who brought up the idea," she reminded him.

His lips thinned. "Believe me, cupcake. I'm well aware of my own mistakes."

She had to wait out the unwanted sting of that. And it didn't matter what his responsibility in the situation was. She'd been the one to offer her assistance to Tara and she planned to honor her words. "I don't intend to let her down."

He leaned a few inches closer. "You heard her. She needs permanent help. Not just someone who'll play at it for a week or two before getting bored."

She didn't back away. "I don't suppose it even occurs to you that I might need this, too?"

"Need?" His lips twisted. "What could working in a small-town shop get you that you couldn't buy a hundred times over?"

Her throat tightened and she wished that she'd just let his underwhelming opinion of her pass. "Obviously nothing that you'd ever understand." To him, she was just a useless "cupcake."

His eyes narrowed even more, but fortunately he was given no opportunity to respond since his mother announced that they'd all adjourn to the family room while the kids cleared the table. The kids in question, Eli and his sister, Megan, groaned about the task, but as Sydney left the table and was joined by Tara—who tucked her arm through hers as if they were lifelong friends—she noticed that their grumbling didn't keep them from their assignment.

"So," Tara was saying, "do you have any kind of retail experience?"

Sydney was glad that Derek had been waylaid by his father in the dining room and wasn't close enough to hear. "Afraid not. If you want to change your mind, I certainly won't blame you."

Tara squeezed her arm. "Please. *I* didn't have any retail experience when I started out." She laughed a little. "If I had, I would have known that a shop like Classic Charms would have an abysmal chance of succeeding in Weaver. Sometimes blissful ignorance is a blessing. What I didn't know didn't hurt me." She looked up at Sydney. "You know, J.D. never mentioned how much you look like Jake. The resemblance is really quite remarkable."

Even from the emptied dining room, Derek could hear Sydney's sudden laughter.

The sound of it seemed to slide down his spine, making heat collect at the base.

"What's going on between you and Jake's little sister?"

"I'm thirty-two, Dad." Derek gave his father a mild look. "Wouldn't worry about it if I were you."

"I'll worry when she's a guest in our home," Matthew returned just as mildly.

Thirty-two or not, Derek was still Matthew's son; it

was clear from his father's tone that he meant business. "We might have gotten off to the wrong start," he reluctantly allowed. "But we got it straight."

His father lifted a disbelieving brow. "Did you, now."

Derek grimaced. "Okay. So we're working on getting it straight."

Matthew just continued looking at him.

Derek exhaled, irritated. Megan and Eli were carrying the last of the dishes out to the kitchen. "She gets under my skin," he muttered.

"Is that so?"

Derek didn't like the sudden glint of amusement in his father's eyes. "She doesn't belong here in Weaver."

"Better be careful, son," he warned. "I once thought that about your mother."

Derek snorted. "There's a big difference between Mom and Sydney."

"Well," Matthew considered, "your mother is a beautiful redhead. Still. And Sydney is a beautiful brunette."

"That's not what I mean."

"You don't think Sydney's beautiful? Had your eyes tested lately?"

"Hell." Derek tossed his hands up. "Of course she's beautiful." She was a gut-wrenching sexy version of grown-up Snow White from the blue-black hair that hugged her ivory face to that leather number that hugged her long-legged, deadly curves. "I know Jake wants his sister to stay in Weaver. But she's not going to."

"She tell you that herself?"

"She doesn't have to. *Look* at her."

Matthew smiled outright. "I did, but your mom noticed and then I had the pleasure of her kicking me under the table."

Derek groaned. "Jesus, Dad."

"I'm married, not blind." He closed his hand over Derek's shoulder and his smile died. "She's Jake's sister and that makes her family by extension. Blaming her for getting under your skin is about as useful as blaming a compass for pointing north. And blaming her for something she hasn't done—and might never do—just because that's what Renée did, is just as pointless."

Derek's shoulders stiffened. "This isn't about Renée." He hadn't mentioned his ex-fiancée's name in a long while, and didn't want to now, either.

He still couldn't think about her and what she'd done without wanting to break something.

His father just looked at him. "Isn't it?"

"Come on, Sydney! You can do it!"

Sydney stared at the snowbank in front of her.

After dessert, it had been young Megan and Eli who'd volunteered to show her around the Double-C. Sydney had been so relieved that it wasn't going to be Derek who'd be saddled with the chore, that she'd happily agreed to exchange her boots and dress for some borrowed clothes and snow boots. It was only after she'd done so that she'd realized that Derek was still coming along.

By then, it was too late to back out. Particularly when she suspected that's exactly what he wanted her to do.

Despite her misgivings, though, Derek had fallen easily enough into the role of tour guide as they'd tromped around. He'd even refrained from any remotely personal comments, sticking to the topic of the cattle ranch that had been in his family for generations.

As for Sydney, she had little breath left over for comments of her own. Not when they were busy keeping up with the boundless energy Derek's niece and nephew possessed. By the time they'd walked through all of the outbuildings and then all the way out to the nearly frozen swimming hole that had to have been a couple miles away, her chest hurt and the muscles in her thighs were stinging. Despite the hours she spent with her personal trainer, trudging through a few feet of snow for a few hours was a heck of a lot worse than anything that Janine had ever put her through.

But now, if she could ascend the solid-looking snowbank that rose twice as high as her head, it would cut at least a half mile from their trek back.

"You'll never know if you can make it unless you try. But if you're afraid, I'll go back and bring a truck," Derek said beside her.

She gave him a thin glare. He was the other reason she felt determined to get up that snowbank. "And here I thought you were going to manage not to say something insulting. I am not afraid."

He lifted his hands innocently, but the devilish curl on his lips was anything but. "It was just an offer."

"An offer implying I can't climb up that snowbank," she muttered.

"You want me to come down and give you a push from behind?" Eli seemed enthusiastic about the prospect as he looked down at her. He and Megan were already standing at the top.

Megan snorted. "I ought to give *you* a push," she warned.

Sydney managed not to laugh. Over the past few hours, it had become increasingly obvious to her that Eli found her attractive.

"I think I can manage," she told him. Derek's muffled laugh beside her wasn't so easy to ignore. "*You're* not giving me a push, either," she told him under her breath.

"Didn't offer, cupcake. But if you want my hands on

your butt, say the word. We don't have to like each other to want each other."

"Don't flatter yourself," she snapped, but had to stare hard at the sloping snowbank to battle her own imagination. Contemplating the mountain of white was much more comfortable than entertaining any sort of notion involving Derek's hands.

She pulled in another deep breath, then planted the toe of one borrowed boot into the steep bank. Once she got started, the task was less daunting than she'd feared, but she still had snow clinging to her legs and coat by the time she managed to scramble to the top. Eli and Megan lent their aid, grabbing her beneath the arms to help her up the last foot. Even then, Derek still managed to get to the top before she did.

But her annoyance over that fell away when she straightened and dusted off the sticking snow. She couldn't help but catch her breath all over again at the postcard-perfect sight.

Megan clearly understood. "It's pretty, huh?"

"Yes." White-capped mountains loomed in the distance. Spiky winter-bare trees lined a narrow creek bravely winding free of the pristine snow that glistened like diamonds in the dwindling light. In the distance, she could see downward to the back side of the big house where smoke curled from one of the chimneys and golden light spilled from the windows.

She'd traveled the world but had always thought that Forrest's Crossing—despite her love-hate relationship with the place—was one of the most beautiful spots on earth.

But this was just as beautiful in an entirely different way.

Forrest's Crossing was all genteel, Southern charm

from its steepled horse barns and white-fenced paddocks to its perfectly manicured grounds.

This looked like nothing but nearly untouched nature.

Nearly, because there were several tall very modern-looking windmills on the crest of the sharp hill where they stood. They weren't the only modern touch she'd noticed around the ranch, either. Several of the barns and outbuildings they'd toured had obviously been outfitted with solar panels.

"Not exactly the Swiss Alps or wherever you like to while away your winters."

Sydney eyed Derek. He was standing several yards away, but she'd heard him easily, as if even sound traveled more quickly in this pristine land. "No, it isn't. But if you can't see the beauty around you right here, then I feel sorry for you."

His frown was quick and surprised, but fortunately, whatever he would have said went unspoken when Eli piped up. "It's nothin' like where I came from in California, that's for sure," the boy said. Instead of standing there to admire the view, though, he started off in the direction of the house.

After a moment, Derek looked away from her and followed his nephew.

It was, mercifully, all downhill from there.

Sydney looked down at Megan, who was hanging back with her. "You and your brother lived in California?" For some reason, she'd assumed they'd been born and raised in Weaver, though she didn't really know why. Except that they seemed to possess that "we belong here" quality that everyone around here had.

Everyone except for Sydney, of course.

Megan started walking, too, and Sydney fell in step with her. "Eli came from California. I came from Virginia. We're both adopted, 'cept Eli was with Dad since he was a baby."

The dad, Sydney knew, was Max Scalise, the local sheriff. Neither he nor his wife, Sarah, had been at dinner that day, though—according to Megan—they were picking them up later. "And you?"

"They didn't get me until I was eight after my real parents died." Her voice was matter-of-fact.

"I'm sorry."

"I got lucky. Mom and Dad—Sarah and Max, I mean—they're okay. And then they had Benny, too, and it's like he's all of us combined. He's with Mom and Dad this afternoon."

"Ben," Eli called from up ahead. "Benny's for babies."

Megan rolled her eyes. "*Ben* is only four," she yelled at the back of her brother's head.

"And do you have any cousins?" Sydney said casually, watching Derek's back several yards ahead of them. Unlike Eli, Megan and Sydney, his head and hands were bare, though he showed enough human frailty to keep his hands shoved in the pockets of his leather jacket.

"You mean from Uncle Derek?" Megan shook her head. Her voice dropped to a whisper. "He doesn't even got a girlfriend," she confided. "Grandma says it's 'cause he's still pining for Renée." Her whisper dripped over the name. "They were supposed to get married, but they didn't." Without missing a step, she leaned over and grabbed up a handful of snow, packed it together in a ball, and launched it at her brother's back.

It exploded in a splatter and Eli whirled around, scooping up his own ammunition.

Sydney had to swallow her unwelcome curiosity where Derek and his broken engagement were concerned, and dart out of the way or end up in firing range of the missiles as the two youngsters chased each other, whooping and hollering, toward the big house. Even then, she wasn't entirely successful.

And since she couldn't avoid them, she decided to join them, throwing her own inexpertly made snowballs right back. Unfortunately, her aim was off, and she hit Derek, smack in the side of the head.

Her laughter cut off midstream as he slowly turned to look her way.

"Sorry," she said breathlessly. "I was aiming for Eli."

He cocked an eyebrow, giving an exaggerated look to where his nephew was bent nearly in half, laughing wildly. "Is that so?" There was at least ten feet between him and the boy.

Megan dashed over beside Sydney. "Here." She handed one snowball to Sydney. She had another already clasped in her mitten. "We can take him," she said, dancing from one boot to the other in anticipation. "Uncle Derek says he always wins, but not this time."

Derek chuckled outright. "Meggie, babe, you'd better teach your firing mate to have better aim, then. And warn her that I never like to lose."

"If you're six feet off," Megan said from the side of her mouth, "just aim six feet over."

It wasn't the worst advice Sydney had ever had and before Derek stopped chuckling, she launched the well-packed snowball.

It missed his head only because he ducked at the last minute to avoid it.

But Megan's snowball hit him square in the chest and Sydney couldn't help but laugh.

Until Megan's hand slid into hers and tugged. "Yeah, that was good," she said hurriedly, "but now we gotta *run!*" And she took off toward the big house, fairly dragging Sydney behind her.

They were both out of breath when they reached the house and fell back against the porch rail.

Eli and Derek finished closing the distance. Neither one was holding any snowballs.

"Chicken," Eli accused Megan when he reached her, and clucking and flapping his arms, he ran into the house with his sister hot on his heels.

Which left Sydney alone with Derek for the first time since she'd arrived that day.

Was he still pining for Renée?

She folded her arms across her chest, stomping out the thought. "Thanks for the tour," she said politely. "You were very…informative."

The corners of his lips quirked. She wasn't sure if it was amusement or something else.

"I grew up here," was all he said.

"Yes. Well, thanks again." Her sense of awkwardness was growing by leaps and bounds. "I know you were pretty much forced into it."

He seemed to sigh a little. "You might as well know that there's not much I get forced—" he began, only to jerk his head around when his mother spoke from the house.

"Anyone for some hot coffee?" Sydney could barely make out Jaimie's face, with the light spilling out from behind her. But her auburn hair glowed as if it possessed a halo.

Sydney's throat suddenly felt tight yet again. "I'm afraid I should pass," she told the older woman. "I want to get back before it's completely dark." She didn't want to admit that she didn't have complete faith in her little car.

"Derek, why don't you take her home?" Jaimie switched

tracks without hesitation. "She's right to be worried about the roads. When the light goes, it's dark as pitch and I know there aren't any lights out by that little cabin she's using."

"No, no," Sydney said quickly. "I'll be fine. And I'll need my car in the morning to get to Tara's shop, anyway," she added quickly.

"I'll follow her," Derek said abruptly.

"That's perfect, honey. So you *will* have time for a hot drink before you go." Clearly satisfied, Jaimie disappeared into the house, the storm door squeaking softly as it closed after her.

Sydney turned on Derek. "This is not necessary."

"There's no point in arguing with her."

"Fine. Then she can think you're following me, but you don't have to actually do it. I'm not an idiot. I found my way out here," she said, hating that her voice sounded tight, "I can find my way back."

He shrugged. "Don't put so much stock in it, cupcake. I live out the same way as the cabin."

She might as well have been a balloon pricked with a needle, she felt so abruptly deflated. "Oh."

"Oh," Derek returned, his voice low and mocking. And then he pulled his hand from his pocket and pushed the snowball he was holding against her neck.

She cried out and jumped back, trying to shake the icy stuff free and only succeeding in sending more of it inside her coat.

He just stood there smiling. "I tried to warn you, cupcake. I never like to lose."

Chapter Four

"Impossible man."

The next morning, Sydney was still cursing Derek Clay.

No amount of attempts on her part to duplicate his efforts with the old furnace had been successful and the thought of going another day without heat was no more appealing than just giving up and going back to Georgia where everyone seemed to think she belonged.

There was no point in calling the same repair service that she'd called two days ago. Once the speckle-faced kid the company sent had finally shown up a few hours after Derek had, she'd ascertained that the boy was no more knowledgeable than she was, and that he only had his job because his mother's fourth husband happened to be the owner of the handyman service.

Which left Sydney with two choices.

Use the phone number that Jake had left her for the

Double-C ranch or figure out a way to handle the matter herself. Even though she was no more certain of success than she'd ever been, she chose the latter.

She had a fireplace, didn't she?

Which is why she was now breathing in air so bitterly cold it made her chest hurt, a long-handled ax clenched against her blistering palm as she stared at an upended log, balanced on an ancient-looking tree stump.

In theory, she knew how to split a log.

In practice, however, it was more challenging than she'd expected. She had only a few hours before she needed to drive into town and meet Tara at the shop and that time was rapidly dwindling as she fought with the logs.

There was an enormous stack of them under a shelter behind the cabin, obviously there to be used once the supply of split firewood was depleted.

Which Sydney had already done.

Problem was, none of the whole pieces would fit into the fireplace. She knew, because she'd already tried.

Ergo her somewhat pathetic attempt at splitting more.

She threw her head back and stared up at the pale blue sky. The sun had been up for only an hour or so. She took a deep, painful breath and let it out. It clouded around her face.

"Why did you move here, Jake?"

But there was no one there to hear her breathless question.

And it was moot, anyway.

Jake had moved to Wyoming because he'd fallen in love.

Sydney had moved to Wyoming because she'd fallen *out* of love. Not that she'd ever really been in love with

Antoine in the first place. Or Jonathan before him. Or Bennett before him.

She closed her eyes and shook her head.

She was through with Antoine and all the others who'd been just like him. No more men who were just like her father.

No more men, period. Not for a long, long while.

So why couldn't she get Derek Clay out of her head?

"New start," she muttered, looking back at the thick piece of tree that had resisted the point of her ax three times already. "New—" she lifted the ax over her shoulder "—*start*." She swung it down, burying the edge of the blade about an inch into the concrete-hard wood.

The impact jammed through her shoulders and she unpeeled her aching hand from the wooden handle.

The ax stayed put, angling out from the log, which might have been dented enough to hold the wedge-shaped blade, but looked no more likely to split into halves than it ever had.

Her palms were stinging and she let out a defeated breath.

Maybe she could buy firewood at one of the stores in town, at least enough to get her through a day or two. She knew there was a Shop-World—a big box type of store on the other side of town—and even though she'd never personally shopped at one, she wasn't so out of touch that she didn't know they were supposed to carry nearly everything. She would drive out there after she was done for the day at Classic Charms.

Since the plan didn't involve calling anyone for rescue, it was the best she could think of for now until she decided what to do about the faulty furnace. Jake certainly wouldn't care if she had it replaced, and she knew she could call him in California for advice.

But she didn't want advice. She wanted…needed…to handle her life herself.

Leaving the ax where it was, she loaded the miserly few pieces of wood that she had managed to break apart into her arms and carried them inside.

The fire in the fireplace was barely clinging to life and she debated the merits of adding one of her hard-won pieces now, or saving them until later. In the end, comfort won out. She still had to shower, and she didn't relish getting dressed without some bit of heat. She stoked the fire into life again with the iron poker and once the flame was snapping and licking hungrily around its fresh fuel, she fit the heavy fireplace screen back into place and removed her cashmere coat.

Flecks of dirt and wood splinters clung to the entire front of it, but she was simply too tired just then to care. She tossed it over one arm of the ugly couch, then sat down to pull off her flat-heeled riding boots. Until she got to town to buy more suitable boots for the snow, at the moment, they were the best she had with her. She dropped them on the braided rug and wiggled her stockinged toes in front of the fire until some feeling came back into them.

Then, because there was no choice, she left the comfort of the minimally warm living area for the single bedroom and the minuscule bathroom on the other side of it. The bathroom wasn't so bad. Fortunately, the water heater worked much more efficiently than the furnace and she had a nearly endless supply of hot water. Enough to heat the confines of the sparsely furnished bathroom with enough steam that undressing to take a shower wasn't an exercise in torture.

So she took a hot shower, long enough to leave her toes actually looking a little pruned before she dried off and covered them once again in two layers of socks. She pulled on a pair of charcoal-gray slacks and added a long-sleeved cashmere black turtleneck and a safari-style, gray canvas jacket that she'd gotten in Africa a few years ago.

The blisters on her palms made even the task of dressing and blow-drying her hair an effort, but she didn't have any bandages on hand, either.

A trek to the store later was definitely in order since she had no housekeeper here to take care of such matters for her. Boots. Wood. Bandages. She ticked off a mental list.

She finished eating her breakfast of dry toast and herbal tea and by that time, the fire had settled down to a comfortable red glow. Since the cast-iron fireplace screen weighed a small ton, she didn't worry about a log falling out and setting the place on fire while she was gone.

For the first time in two days, she pulled her cell phone out of her purse and glanced at the screen. No messages from Antoine. Not that she'd expected any.

He'd been pretty plain when he'd told her he wasn't interested in any sort of future. Particularly now. Nor were there any messages from anyone else.

Certainly none from one Derek Clay.

"Why would you expect otherwise?" she asked herself. And had no answer.

She sighed a little and dropped the phone in her purse, pulled out her car keys and braved the cold outside to attempt shaking the worst of the wood flecks from her coat before pulling it on and heading across the crunchy ground toward the shed. She couldn't bear the thought of her kid gloves against her palms—they'd been worse than nothing when she'd tried wearing them while chopping wood—and left them where they were, shoved in her coat pockets.

Twenty minutes later, she was still sitting in her car, inside the shed, because the engine wouldn't catch. It wouldn't even turn over and feeling that further efforts would be absolutely futile, she gave up.

So far, the day was off to a fabulous start. At this rate she wouldn't be getting to work, much less any store afterward. Her eyes itched with tears that were dangerously close.

What are you doing here, Sydney?

But if she let herself cry now, over a stupid car that was temperamental on the best of days, then she really was just as useless as she'd always been told.

She blew out a long breath and flipped the hood latch, then climbed out of the car. But when she was standing there staring down at the mysteries of the car engine, she wondered why she was bothering. She knew as much about cars as she did about furnaces. She just put gas in and let her longtime family mechanic take care of everything else.

She ignored the nausea tugging at her coattails and tried to think practically. She'd have to call Tara and tell her she couldn't make it yet. Palatable or not, it was the simple truth.

She grimaced and slammed the hood shut. And her morning took another sharp turn when she walked out of the shed and saw Derek Clay's muddy pickup truck driving toward her.

Her nerves jangled and she shoved her hands into her pockets.

He *had* followed her home the night before. When she'd turned up the drive toward the cabin, he'd flashed his lights once, and kept right on driving.

She'd been almost pathetically relieved that he hadn't

followed her up to the cabin. He was irritating. Annoying. Confusing.

And she just didn't know how to deal with him.

Now, she ducked her chin beneath her coat collar and waited until he'd pulled up nearly beside her.

Down rolled the window. Out stared his green eyes. "Aren't you supposed to be at Tara's shop by now?"

She jerked her chin upward. She hadn't cried in front of anyone in more years than she could count and she wasn't about to start by doing it now, particularly in front of this man.

"I'll pay you fifty dollars for a ride into town," she said flatly. "Maybe you can use it to buy yourself a decent razor."

His eyebrow peaked and he angled his head, looking toward the shed. The door was still thrown wide, revealing her little car sitting inside. "Car problems?"

"Yes or no?"

She could see his thumb beating against the steering wheel and after a moment, he shrugged. "Fifty bucks is fifty bucks."

She didn't give herself an opportunity to second-guess herself. "I have to get my purse."

Derek watched her as she strode around the front of his truck, back toward the shed.

Even hunched the way she was inside the calf-length coat she clutched around her, she moved gracefully. Her long stride quickly covered the distance, and then just as quickly she was heading back toward him, shaking her head against the glossy black strands of hair that blew across her eyes.

His hands tightened around the steering wheel as he

waited for her to open the passenger door and climb up inside. He wasn't offering any help. No way. No how.

He'd decided the day before, after their little snowball fight, that keeping his hands to himself where she was concerned was the wisest thing all around.

His reasoning was simple. He didn't want anything from her that wouldn't get him into a heap of discomfort with the family.

He didn't mind discomfort…if it was worth it.

Which meant he'd just have to get over wondering what Sydney would be like in bed.

Cold air blew through the cab as she opened the door and quickly pulled herself up onto the high seat. Without looking at him, she closed the door and clicked the seat belt into place. "Does the wind ever stop blowing?"

He put the truck in gear and turned back the way he'd come. "Not very often." Fortunately, for him, since the business he owned specialized, lucratively, in designing alternative energy systems. "What's with the car?"

She still didn't look his way. Just pointed that narrow, tilted-up, sexy nose straight out the windshield. "It doesn't like the cold any more than I do."

"Then take it, and you, back home."

"Where I belong?"

He turned out onto the empty highway. "You said it, not me."

"Maybe not *to* me. But you're thinking it." She folded her arms tightly over her chest and even as long-legged as she was, managed to look small. Vulnerable.

Dammit.

Snobby and high-maintenance, maybe. But vulnerable?

A stream of curses flew through his head. He did not want to deal with vulnerable.

"J.D. grew up here," he said abruptly. "And Jake's only

signed on here 'cause they're attached at the hip now." He veered around a slow-moving snowplow. "If you want to visit, fine. I get it. He's your brother. But why move here? Even if you found some sense and stayed somewhere more comfortable than that cabin, there's still nothing easy about this place. It'll chew you up and spit you out if you're not prepared for it."

She angled her chin, sliding a narrow look around the wing of black hair cupping her cheek. "I'm guessing that you're *not* an official member of the Weaver Welcoming Committee?"

He didn't smile, and her lips tightened. "My aunt lives here, too," she reminded him. "In fact, I have more family living in Weaver now than anywhere else. Charlotte's on the road with Forco business more often than she's home in Georgia. Besides *your* family, what's Weaver got to offer you?"

"That's different."

She huffed and she turned back toward the windshield. "Please."

Even he recognized the absurdity of his own logic. "My business is here. I was born and raised here. I've seen people come and I can recognize the ones who'll end up going."

"Do tell." She sounded bored.

He didn't know why he didn't just drop it. But he plowed on, anyway. "Save yourself the grief and do it sooner rather than later. It's nothing to be ashamed about. Life here just doesn't suit everybody. You're used to…"

"To *what?*"

"*Finer* things," he finally said.

"Being the snob that I am and all," she concluded.

He exhaled and slowed as he entered the edges of town.

"I'm sorry I called you a snob, all right? I shouldn't have said it but you just—"

She lifted an eyebrow, giving him a look.

"—rubbed me wrong," he finished.

"That makes two of us who were rubbed all wrong, then, doesn't it?"

He grimaced. "All this rubbin' going on and nobody getting any pleasure out of it."

Her eyes popped wide. "I beg your pardon?"

"Ought to be a law against it."

She just stared.

He stopped at one of the few traffic lights the town possessed. "I'm joking, okay?" Mostly. "Do you *have* a sense of humor lurking behind that pretty face of yours?"

"When something is actually funny," she deadpanned. "How much farther to Tara's shop?"

He pointed. "Just down the road here."

She tucked her hand in her purse, pulled out a folded bill that she tossed on the dashboard and started to push open her door.

"Hold it." He grabbed her hand before she could unsnap her seat belt.

She winced and yanked her hand free.

He knew there was no love lost between them—mostly his doing—but even that wouldn't account for that wince. He grabbed her again, this time around the wrist. "Hold it," he said more gently and turned her palm upward.

She curled her fingers inward. "The light is green."

He didn't even bother to look up from her clenched fist. Her fingernails were cut short and were unpainted. For some reason the lack of artifice surprised him. "What's wrong with your hand?"

"Someone won't let *go* of it," she said pointedly.

"Sydney," he chided softly. "Let me see."

Her jaw slid from one side to the other. Then she exhaled with obvious frustration and opened her palm.

A line of angry blisters stared up at him.

He swore. "How'd you get these?"

Her fingers were already curling up again, as if she could erase the fact that he'd already seen the damage. "None of your business." Her seat belt retracted with a snap and she reached for the door again.

"I'm making it my business."

She looked over her shoulder at him, her sapphire eyes bewildered. "Why?"

Hell if he knew.

But he did.

Vulnerable. It sucked him in whether he wanted it to or not.

"Because both your brother and your aunt are out of town." Even he could hear how cranky he sounded. "*Somebody* obviously has to."

"So who better than a kissin' cousin?" She smiled sarcastically. "Thank you, but I'll pass on this particular pleasure." She pushed open the door, purse in hand, and hopped out.

"How are you going to get back home again?" he asked before she could close the door.

"I'd walk before I'd ask you, that's for certain." She slammed the door shut and jogged away. He saw her start to slip when she went between two of the parked cars nosed up to the curb at an angle, but she caught herself and made it safely to the sidewalk.

Derek rolled down the window and trolled alongside her. "Until you come to your senses, at least buy yourself some snow boots," he called after her.

"And have them clash with the ensemble?" She walked faster.

He followed her a few more doors. They passed several storefronts before reaching the end of the block. "Tara will give you a ride home," he called out when she left the curb to cross the small side street. "And if she can't, she can call someone who can." He'd do it himself if he didn't have business in Casper all day. "And make sure you get some bandages on those hands. You'll be worse than miserable if those blisters get infected."

She reached the other curb and stopped on her heel to face him, her hands on her hips that—even draped in a cashmere coat—looked narrow. He rolled to a stop, glad that there was no traffic to speak of.

"Stop talking as if I'm incompetent!" She all but stomped her fancy boot. "I can take care of myself!" The bottom of her coat whirled around her legs as she took off down the block again.

He hit the gas enough to catch up to her once more. "Thought you were going to Tara's shop."

She threw her hands up and sent him a glare across her shoulder. "I *am*. Obviously."

"Really? So you're taking the long way around, for some reason?"

"What?"

He pointed. "You passed the shop about three doors back."

He saw the ire in her eyes as she whirled around to look.

"Bandages," he called out one more time.

She gave him a glare, then stomped away.

He sat there watching in his rearview mirror until she'd disappeared through the fancy glass door of Classic Charms. And only thought to roll up the windows again and get moving when one of the sheriff's department vehicles stopped behind him and hit the horn.

He gave an absent wave at the officer and was just glad it wasn't his own brother-in-law, Max, behind the wheel. He wouldn't have lived it down.

Sydney wasn't sure how she managed to shove the capital-A Annoyance that was Derek Clay out of her thoughts when she entered Tara's shop.

Maybe it was the fact that the shop was an absolutely unexpected delight, from the Christmas tree decorated with enticing bits of delicate lingerie and chocolates hanging from ribbons that stood near the front window, to the leather saddle bearing an oversize teddy bear inside an old-fashioned red telephone booth near the mahogany sales counter, to the racks of beautifully displayed clothing. There were also paintings on the walls and little groupings of furniture just inviting a person to come in and have a seat.

The entire effect was charming, and aside from a few items, Sydney quickly realized with Tara's tutelage, all of it was for sale. Nothing went to waste.

If she'd worried about Tara changing her mind about Sydney's lack of qualifications, she'd worried for nothing. The other woman was patience itself, never seeming to lose her smile as the two of them dealt with a surprisingly steady stream of customers. It was only after lunch—which Tabby delivered since she worked at the nearby diner where Tara had ordered it—that Sydney's new boss finally tossed herself down onto an oversize leather chair and put up her feet.

"Sit down," Tara ordered, waving at the chair's twin positioned adjacent to her. "There's always a lull around this time and you'll be on your feet plenty enough as it is."

Sydney's feet weren't particularly bothering her. She

was accustomed to being on her feet since most evenings spent with Antoine had usually involved socializing with artists and collectors at one function or another. And she was itching to study the jewelry that was in a display case alongside the counter more closely. But she sat.

Tara's hands were folded atop her belly. It didn't seem possible, but Sydney could have sworn that the other woman's baby bulge looked twice the size as it had the day before.

And Sydney could hardly tear her eyes away from it.

"So have I already bored you to tears with shop details?"

"No!" Startled, Sydney sat forward. "It's been fascinating."

Tara's brows rose and she chuckled a little. "Well, there was a time when it was all that kept me going." She smoothed her hand over her stomach, that seemingly perpetual smile still on her face. "Then along came Axel... and his babies."

Sydney knew the other woman well enough now to recognize that the smile wasn't the least bit false. Tara Clay was obviously happy with her life.

"When are you due?"

"End of March, thereabouts." She tucked her nut-brown hair behind her ear. "So, if I haven't bored you stiff already, let's talk salary. What were you expecting?"

Sydney swallowed, suddenly uncomfortable. "Tara, I don't need a salary." She didn't want to point out the obvious, but this woman *did* know Jake. Of course she knew the kind of wealth the Forrests possessed.

"Well, I'm not letting you work here four days a week like we agreed on if you're not getting paid," Tara countered easily. "You can do whatever you want with the money. It's not going to be much," she warned laughingly. "The shop's doing well, but not well compared to Forrest standards." She lifted her shoulders. "What have you done with your earnings from other positions you've held?"

"I've never had any other paid positions." Feeling awkward, she pushed out of the chair and wandered over to the counter. The mahogany was as smooth as glass, but warm in a way that glass could never be. "This looks like it belongs in the bar from some John Wayne movie set."

"Well, it did come from a bar," Tara allowed, sounding amused. "Pretty sure the Duke never set his elbows on it, though. So what sort of work *have* you done?"

She'd known that the topic would come up again. She caught herself from picking at one of the bandage strips that Tara had given her for her hands. "Racehorses and art." She looked at Tara and shook her head. "I warned you that you'll want someone with more qualifications. The *truth* is—" Her throat tightened and she swallowed hard. "The truth is, I've never really done anything. Nothing that was worth getting paid for."

Though Antoine had implied that she'd been amply compensated by him for her "services." The thought was bitter. The nauseating feeling that accompanied it was something that she hoped would pass more quickly.

Tara's smile finally died.

She pulled her feet down and sat forward, as far as her belly would allow. Her eyes were soft. "I think you're probably not giving yourself enough credit. Tell me about the racehorses. I know your family owns a lot of them, and that's how J.D. and Jake met."

Sydney nodded. "At Forrest's Crossing. She started out there as a groom and worked up to assistant trainer before she came back to Wyoming. Jake ended up following, obviously." Now, her brother and sister-in-law were establishing Crossing West right outside Weaver. Thoroughbreds would always be part of Jake's world, but with J.D. they were also establishing a horse rescue. "I've found us a few horses over the years. But it was always up to Jake to negotiate the deals. I sit on the board at Forco, but don't do anything except nod when expected, and the only thing my art history degree got me was chairing a few charity auctions."

"Sounds like a life that most shopgirls would dream of having."

Sydney made a face. "Not if they knew what it was really like."

"Well." Tara was smiling again. "The only requirement *I* have is a willingness to work, and you've convinced me that you have that." She leaned back again and patted her belly. "I was becoming afraid that once this little one came, I'd have to close the shop altogether." She beamed. "But now you'll be here."

Thoughts of Derek swam into her head all over again, bumping into the knowledge that there was still another important detail that Tara needed to know.

Eventually.

When Sydney was ready to talk about it.

Her index finger picked at the edge of the loose bandage strip. "Derek…thinks I'd be better off back home in Georgia."

"And you care what Derek thinks?" Tara's smile took on a speculative cast. "How…interesting."

"No!" Sydney pushed her hands behind her back and leaned over the jewelry case. A small part of her mind noticed how exquisitely unique the pieces were, but the rest of her mind was busy trying to shove the annoying man out of her head. And failing. "I was just making a comment."

"We all noticed you two were thick as thieves yesterday. Poor guy can't keep his eyes off you."

Sydney jerked upright and whirled. "*Poor* guy? He's the most irritating person I've ever met in my life!"

"I've thought that very thing a time or two about Axel." Tara leaned back once more, stroking her belly and looking supremely content. "And now look at me."

Sydney smiled, too, but it was weak in comparison.

She couldn't help but think that Tara would be less inclined to entertain the idea of romantic possibilities between her cousin-in-law and her newest employee if she knew that she wasn't the *only* pregnant woman in the room.

Chapter Five

She was the most annoying woman he'd ever met.

So why hadn't he been able to get Sydney Forrest out of his thoughts since that morning?

The question was still plaguing Derek that evening as he finally headed home for the day. The sun had been down for hours.

Had she hated her day at Tara's shop?

His fingers tightened around the steering wheel as he passed Colbys bar. Maybe if he pulled in there, had a beer and a game of pool with whoever was around, he'd get that woman out of his head. He could call his cousin, Casey. See if he was back in town yet. He was always up for suds and cues.

Instead of turning in at the familiar haunt—crowded even now on a Monday evening—he kept on driving, leaving the lights of the town behind as he picked up speed, barreling through the night on the empty highway.

He'd stopped by her place that morning on his way out of town to check on the furnace again. He had spare keys for all of the buildings on Jake's property since he was designing the systems to meet the energy needs for Crossing West.

But he'd expected *her* to be long gone.

He knew from Axel that Tara had driven her home after they'd finished for the day, because his cousin had mentioned it when Derek called him about a pool competition they were considering signing up for at Colbys. Ax hadn't been fooled by the pretext, though, and his cousin had found it pretty hilarious that Derek had even tried.

But then Axel always did have a strange sense of humor.

Derek was just trying to follow through on his promise to Jake to look after things around their place while they were gone. It made sense. He lived the closest.

And the "things" at Crossing West now included Sydney.

He was satisfied with the soundness of his logic.

He just wasn't satisfied with the way he was bugged by it.

Not it.

Her.

Swearing a blue streak, he made a U-turn and sped back a half mile until he reached the turnoff for her place. The lights were visible even from a distance; then again, unless she'd managed to get her car started, where else would she be but there? Her distaste for asking for help was as plain as the sexy nose on her face. Paying for it was what she preferred.

The fifty-dollar bill that she'd given him was proof of that.

He parked in front of the log cabin and studied it. There

was a thin line of smoke curling from the chimney—he was glad that he'd managed to have the chimney cleaned when Jake told Derek that his sister wanted to stay there and not at the main house.

Jake had said simply, "Who can explain my sister?" when Derek had questioned her choice since the cabin had sat unoccupied for the better part of a decade. As it was, they'd had only a few days' notice to get anything done before she'd arrived in town and Jake headed off for his vacation.

Blowing out a breath, he left the truck and went to the door and knocked. He could hear faint music from inside—new country, which was vaguely surprising since she seemed more uptight-classical to him—but there was no motion that he could detect behind the ancient curtain hanging in the small window next to the door. He knocked again and when there was still no answer, he headed back to his truck and retrieved his heavy-duty flashlight. There was still no response over at the cabin so he walked beyond it to the shed and shoved aside the door, playing the beam of his flashlight inside.

Her toy car was inside.

He closed the door again and turned back toward the cabin. The beam of his flashlight fell across the tumble of logs spilling out haphazardly from the cord he'd stacked himself before she'd arrived. And the rack he'd filled with dried and split wood next to the cabin was completely empty.

Which meant she'd gone through a helluva lot of wood in a short amount of time.

He bypassed the wood and went back to the door, knocking harder. "Sydney, open up."

Still, there was no answer.

It was way too far to the main house for her to have

tried to walk. Irritation warred with concern and he tried the knob.

He didn't even have to get the set of keys from the truck since the door was unlocked. Not sure if he'd be asking for an object thrown at his head, he cautiously stepped inside.

His gaze skated over the modern paintings she'd hung above the couch; they looked as out of place now as they had the first time he'd seen them. A bowl of half-eaten cereal sat on the metal footlocker serving as a coffee table. The music was coming from the oversize radio sitting on top of the equally old-fashioned television that sat in one corner. And the fire in the fireplace was barely alive.

The room itself, he realized when he closed the door behind him and started to shrug out of his coat, was twenty degrees colder than it should have been. He left his coat on and crossed to the fireplace. There was only one piece of wood left in the bin beside the hearth and it looked as if it had been attacked by alien teeth. Beavers would have made a neater job of chewing.

He jammed the jagged piece onto the embers hard enough to unleash fresh sparks and nudged the screen back in place.

The door to the dark bedroom was ajar.

"Sydney?" It occurred to him that she might be sleeping, and the last thing he wanted to do was startle the life out of some sleeping woman by showing up at her bedside. Moving quietly, just in case, he nudged the door wider, letting some of the light from the living area in.

"Sydney?" He still couldn't see much beyond the foot of the bed. He flipped on the flashlight and trained the strong beam on the floor, cautiously letting it creep up the side of the bed. "You okay?"

The only thing the stronger light revealed was the washed-out color of the rumpled quilt covering the bed.

Unless she was hiding in the closet, the only place left was the bathroom.

"Sydney," he called her name in a voice so loud that she couldn't fail to hear it unless she was unconscious. "It's Derek. I'm taking a look at your furnace."

Sure enough, the bathroom door flew open, and Sydney—wet hair pushed back from her pale face—stood in the beam of his flashlight. Her hand flew up to shade her eyes. "*What* do you think you're doing?" Her voice was practically a shriek.

He clicked off the flashlight. "Sorry. Hard as it might be to believe, I didn't want to scare you."

She leaned against the doorjamb. Her hand dropped from her eyes to the base of her throat. "Too late." She sounded breathless. "Do you always make a habit of breaking and entering?"

"No breaking, cupcake, considering the door was completely unlocked. You might want to rethink that, by the way. Weaver's a pretty quiet place, but you're not far off the highway, and you are a woman alone."

"Would a lock have kept you out?" Her voice turned hopeful.

"No. I have a set of keys from your brother."

Despite the darkness separating them, he could feel the glare she gave him.

"I suppose you want me to give you back the key."

"You think?"

"When did the furnace quit again?"

She exhaled noisily. "The *key?*"

He turned on his heel and went out to his truck, found the appropriate key and took it back inside. She still hadn't emerged from her bathroom. He set the key next to the bowl of soggy cereal and opened the utility door to kneel in front of the furnace.

The pilot light was dead again. Even if he got it going, he suspected it would quickly fail. If he had the entire thing pulled, he could have it replaced with a more efficient unit within a day. His mind quickly ran through schedules and technicians, looking for an opening, and not really finding one. He'd have to put Millie on the task. His secretary was a miracle worker when it came to fitting together the puzzle pieces of the jobs on their plates.

"*Why* won't you leave me alone?"

He rose to his feet and looked at her. Beautiful or not, she looked as gray and washed out as an old dishcloth, and he frowned at her. "Are you feeling okay?"

She nodded once—a nonverbal lie if there ever was one, he figured—and turned away to sit on the couch and drag an afghan over herself. The pants she'd been wearing that morning had been exchanged for a pair of narrow black jeans. Combined with the black turtleneck that hugged her torso in a way he couldn't help but notice, and her water-slick hair, her pallor was only accentuated.

"When's the last time you ate something? And I'm not talking about a half a bowl of cereal," he added when she gave a pointed look at the bowl on the footlocker in front of her.

"I had lunch with Tara. She ordered something from that place where Tabby works."

"Ruby's?"

"That's it." She didn't look at him as she pulled the afghan up to her neck. "And I'm not hungry."

He crossed the room and picked up the bowl, waving it toward her. "Who would be, when you're looking at this?"

She closed her eyes and looked away, then suddenly threw the afghan aside and bolted from the couch.

A second later, he heard the bathroom door slam closed. The sound of her retching was plain even through the door.

He muttered an oath and dumped the cereal in the trash and washed out the bowl, leaving it to dry on the kitchen counter. Then he went through the bedroom and pushed open the bathroom door.

Her hand shot up, staving him off. "Get out!" But even her demand lacked demand. She was huddled on the floor, her cheek resting on the edge of the claw-footed bathtub.

He ignored the hand and grabbed a washcloth off the hook beside the sink and wet it down. He folded it up then sat on the closed lid of the commode near her and pressed the cloth to her forehead.

She closed her eyes but tears crept from the corners. "Can't you just leave me alone?"

He could see the shivers racking her shoulders and he didn't bother answering the obvious. "Do you think you have a fever?" Her forehead didn't feel particularly hot to him when he pulled away the wet cloth to press his palm against it, but then again he didn't go around feeling a lot of foreheads for fevers. It was just something his mom had always done. He put the cloth back in place.

"No." Her voice was nearly soundless.

"How long have you been—" he nearly said puking "—sick?" he amended, thinking his usual term would have offended her sensibilities. "Do you want me to call a doctor? There're two right in the family."

She pressed her hand over his on the wet cloth and for a second—despite the situation—he actually lost his train of thought.

Then she was shifting away from him, and he let his

hand slip from beneath hers. She braced her other hand on the side of the tub and pushed to her feet. She rinsed her face and mouth. "I don't need a doctor," she muttered, and went into the bedroom. "It was probably something I ate."

He followed. He wasn't aware that anyone had ever gotten sick from food prepared at Ruby's. Nor was he so sure that she didn't need medical attention as he watched her practically crawl onto the mattress, pulling the quilt up around her ears. But one thing he did know. The cold temperature inside the cabin wasn't helping her any.

He went into the living room and grabbed the afghan, then took it back into the bedroom. He spread it over her. "You'd be warmer on the couch by the fire."

"I tried that last night," she said. "Too many broken springs."

He sat down on the side of the bed, feeling the shape of her legs that were drawn up tightly against his hip. "So the furnace was out last night, too," he concluded and sighed. "No wonder you're going through firewood at the speed of light. Sydney, why didn't you just tell me earlier?"

"Because I don't need you rescuing me. I don't need anyone rescuing me." She turned onto her other side, presenting him with her back. "I'm *not* incompetent."

"I'm getting the feeling you're trying to convince yourself of that more than anyone else. I've never said you were."

"Right. You just think it. *Cupcake.*" Her voice was muffled. "Like everyone else in my life."

He frowned down at her. "Everyone else, who?"

"It doesn't matter anymore."

He waited for her to say more but she didn't. And after a moment, aware that he was too close to dropping his hand on top of the blanketed bump that was her, he got up from the bed and went back into the living room.

He eyed the empty wood bin and sighed. She'd obviously tried chopping the firewood herself, which explained the state of the piece he'd added to the fire.

It was burning brightly now, but he knew it wouldn't be enough to last through the night. And it needed to burn a lot more brightly if the warmth was going to spread into the bedroom.

He went out to his truck yet again and found a pair of work gloves in his tool box, got his flashlight, and went around to the woodpile. He knew there was a switch for a floodlight somewhere on the corner of the cabin, and he searched around for a while until he found it. Then, with the area between the cabin and the shed illuminated, he made short work of splitting enough logs into quarters to get through the night.

He had nothing against splitting logs by hand; he'd been doing it since he was a kid. But he couldn't imagine Sydney doing it. When morning came, he'd either bring her an automatic splitter that she could use or bring a load of wood from his place that was already split. He would have done it before now if she'd have just said the furnace had quit again. He was more annoyed with himself, though, for not foreseeing the problem when he'd known the furnace was barely hanging on.

For now, though, he settled for carrying a night's supply inside, which he stacked quietly inside the wood bin. He added a few more pieces to the fire, and once he'd stoked it into a decent blaze, he finally shrugged out of his coat and sank down on the couch.

He winced.

She hadn't been joking about the broken springs in the

couch and he thought a little longingly of his king-size bed at home.

But leaving her alone when she was sick wasn't even a consideration and he knew for a fact that she'd split a vein if he suggested going to his place. Even if the old house did possess four bedrooms and three baths, one with a bathtub large enough for two people to roll around in.

So he yanked off his boots and let them drop on the floor beside the couch, then propped his feet on the foot-locker, and slouched down on the only portion of the couch that didn't seem to be filled with bulges and broken springs.

She could have chosen to stay anywhere she wanted. Yet she was determined to stick it out in this cabin. Proving, for whatever reason, and to whomever she needed to prove it to, that she *could.*

He didn't know what was driving her, but he had to give her credit for one thing.

Stubbornness.

It was at least one thing they had in common.

Warmth.

Blessed, wonderful warmth.

Sydney sprawled in the too-soft bed and soaked up the sensation for several minutes before she gingerly turned onto her back.

Despite her caution, though, the nausea that had overtaken her the night before returned with a vengeance, and she practically fell off the bed as she rushed to the bathroom, losing what little contents of her stomach that she had left to lose before curling in a ball on the braided rug that covered part of the wooden floor.

"Still at it, I see."

She closed her eyes tightly, wishing that she could

simply disappear, since it was apparent that *he* wouldn't. "What time is it?"

"Just after six."

Worse and worser. She managed not to groan. "You stayed all night?" *Please, please say "no."*

"Someone had to keep the fire burning."

She heard the rustle of Derek's jeans and then the faucet running. She opened her eyes just in time to see the wet washcloth coming at her forehead. She grabbed it from him. "Thank you, but I'm fine."

"Sure. I could tell that by the way you were worshipping the porcelain goddess again." He sat on the edge of the tub beside her. His feet were bare and he wore only an untucked white T-shirt with the jeans. His hair was tumbling over his forehead and the seemingly perpetual shadow on his jaw was darker than ever.

He looked good enough to eat, if her stomach were only in the mood for it.

She closed her eyes again, not wanting to notice anything about him. Her hand squeezed the wet cloth tightly, which only reminded her of the blisters that lined the pads and base of her fingers. "You cut more firewood?"

"Enough for the night. There're a few pieces left. I'll get you more, though."

"I don't want you to get me more."

"You prefer to freeze?"

"I prefer to take care of myself! I don't know why I can't get you to understand that." Her voice thickened and she pressed her lips together, pushing herself to her feet. But a wave of dizziness hit her and she swayed.

"Hold on, there." Derek's hands shot out and caught her around the waist. "You don't have to rush. Give yourself a minute."

She couldn't do anything but, or else chance toppling over onto her butt or him.

She wasn't sure which would be more embarrassing.

But it didn't matter, anyway, because her stomach rose again, and she leaned urgently past him for the commode.

Humiliation burned more deeply than her empty stomach when she was finished. His hands were still around her, supporting her awkward position and she couldn't look at him as she moved shakily away. She flipped on the water faucet, rinsed her mouth and cupped water over her face.

It was better than letting him see the tears that she couldn't seem to stop, and she'd simply given up on the notion that he'd have the decency to give her some privacy.

"So when's the baby due?" he finally asked.

She went still, staring at the water swirling down the drain of the plain white sink.

"I found the book stuck in the couch," he added quietly.

She couldn't stand there frozen forever, could she? Not even if she wanted to.

She slowly shut off the water. Dried her face with the towel hanging on the back of the door. "It's just a book," she said huskily.

"So you're going to tell me you're *not* pregnant."

The lie was on her lips, but for the life of her, she couldn't get it to come out.

Not answering, she hung the towel on the hook again and left the bathroom. Her legs felt like gelatin but she bypassed the lure of the bed and went into the living area.

A fire was crackling and snapping cozily in the fireplace. Derek's boots were lying on the floor next to the wood bin that now held several pieces of firewood. His shirt was tossed over the arm of the couch.

Her throat felt tight and she kept on going into the kitchen. Even there, he'd left his mark.

The few dishes she'd left in the sink had been washed and put away. A speckled, black coffeepot that she knew had been sitting dusty in a cupboard was shining clean and sitting on top of the stove. She didn't know where he'd gotten the coffee to fill it, but she could smell it.

And her big, glossy everything-about-pregnancy book was sitting on the counter, opened to the third chapter. She'd already read the book through, more than once. The third chapter was "How to conceive without really trying."

Ironic.

She flipped the book closed and filled a glass with water instead of the coffee that she really wanted, and drank it down.

Fortunately, this time her stomach didn't protest.

"What are you? Two, three months along?"

She set the glass in the sink and leaned against the counter behind her and looked at Derek. Did growing up on a ranch enable a man to just know things that others usually didn't?

"Ten weeks," she finally said. "Give or take a day." Truthfully, though, she knew exactly when she'd conceived. It was three months after she'd found Antoine in bed with his assistant. "How could you tell?"

His lips quirked a little. "Aside from this?" He lifted the heavy book a few inches off the counter and dropped it with a thud before grabbing the coffeepot and filling the mug that she hadn't even realized he was holding. "And the way you were driving the white bus in there?"

"I mean how far along I was."

He shrugged. "I've got a sister and a bunch of cousins who've taken to having kids. Isn't hard to figure out." He set down the pot and his gaze ran down her body. "Won't be able to wear those jeans for much longer, I imagine."

She yanked the hem of her sweater over the unfastened button of her jeans and crossed her arms.

Which only seemed to draw his gaze to her breasts that felt excruciatingly sensitive, anyway.

"Is that all you have to say? Don't want to add some unwelcome advice? Some comment about the sins of unwed mothers?"

His lips twisted. "Strangely enough, not this time. Always figured that the baby oughta be more important than the way it comes about." Then he buried his nose in his mug and turned away. After a moment, he waved toward the furnace closet. "I'll make sure that gets replaced for you."

"I can *hire* someone myself. Not that same handyman service I called before, obviously, but I'm sure there's someone around here who can do that sort of work."

At that, he did look back at her, giving her a quizzical look. "That someone would be me. That's one of the things my company does."

She remembered he'd mentioned his business was in Weaver, but she'd assumed he'd meant his family's business. "I thought you worked out at the Double-C."

"I've done that, too, among other things. But I'm an engineer. CLAE—" he spelled it out "—Clay Alternative Energy."

"Windmills and solar panels," she murmured, thinking of what she'd seen at the Double-C the other day. "Weaver have a lot of that sort of work for you?" She couldn't imagine that it did. The town struck her as wholly old-fashioned. "No wonder you have enough time on your hands to keep plaguing me."

"It's not only windmills and panels," he said mildly. "And just because I'm based in Weaver doesn't mean my business ends at the town limits."

Which made her feel just as small as she was acting. "I'm sorry. I don't know why I have a habit of trying to insult you." Her gaze went past him to the fire in the fireplace and the replenished woodbin he was obviously responsible for. It was only because of him that she was able to stand around in her jeans and stocking feet and not feel like she was freezing.

"Yeah, well, right or wrong, I've tossed a few insults of my own," he admitted. He sat on the footlocker and cradled the coffee mug between his palms.

She chewed the inside of her lip. "I, um… I would appreciate it if you didn't tell anyone about…this."

"You being pregnant? Why?" His gaze narrowed between the enviably thick lashes he had. "Not planning to keep it?"

She swallowed the sudden knot in her throat. "That's not it at all. I just want to tell Jake and my aunt after they all get back from California. They should be the first to know."

"Them. Not the baby's father? What about him?"

She ruthlessly squelched the defensiveness that rose inside her. "What about him?"

His gaze narrowed a little more. "Have you told *him?*"

Whether Derek was being surprisingly kind or not, she had no intention of telling him what had occurred between her and Antoine. "This baby is nobody's business but my own." She knew what she was implying—that she hadn't told Antoine—but she considered leaving that misperception in place more palatable than admitting how little regard he'd had for her.

"You didn't make that baby by yourself," Derek pointed out. "He has a right to know. Did he hurt you? Was he violent? Married? What?"

Had Antoine hurt her? If he'd ever had that ability, it had been long gone by the time she'd found him in bed with Trina, or surely she would have reacted differently. Instead, for months she'd ignored the entire event as if it had never occurred. She'd seen them, but they had been too preoccupied to notice her.

And she'd been determined to keep her place in his life. She wasn't going to lose out to some lowly *assistant.* She was a Forrest, for God's sake.

It was only a month ago, when Sydney had told him that she was pregnant, that *he* had broken things off.

And it was only in the time since that she'd had to face some hard truths about herself.

She shook her head. "No. He didn't hurt me. No, he was never violent. And he most certainly was *not* married." He'd had no more interest in that institution than she did. It was one of the reasons why their relationship had worked for the two years that it had.

Derek eyed Sydney, trying to read her expression.

But it was damned hard. She didn't give much away with those blue eyes of hers…not if she could help it.

His fingers tightened around the mug until he was sure it would crack. "Are you in love with him?"

Her eyebrows shot up. "Good grief, no." Then she gave that little smile of hers and her Southern sway became filled with a heavy dose of mockery. "You don't need love to make a baby."

He had in his case.

The thought was bitter.

Renée had believed otherwise, however, and hadn't even *told* him they'd conceived a child. Not when she'd broken off their engagement. Not when she'd left her oil baron daddy's mansion down in Cheyenne in favor of the glittery life she wanted to find in Los Angeles, and not even when she'd aborted that child lest he or she get in the way of her plans.

No. Derek only learned about it after it was all said and done. When he couldn't do anything about it.

He could forgive her for breaking the engagement.

He could even forgive her for not loving him enough to stay.

But he couldn't forgive her for the rest.

"Where is he?" He yanked his thoughts out of the past. "The baby's father?"

"I have no idea where he is, actually. Out of the country, no doubt." Sydney's gaze didn't waver from Derek's. "He's an art dealer. He's based in Atlanta, but he travels extensively."

Derek couldn't help but glance at the paintings hanging on the wall behind him. "And you went with him on his travels? Where he deals in squiggly-lined monstrosities like those?"

"I usually traveled with him, yes. But those *Solieres* have nothing to do with him. I owned them long before we met."

He looked back at her.

Even knowing what he now knew wasn't enough to dull the impact that just looking at her made.

He looked. And he wanted. Pure and simple.

As simple as the fact that she was more off-limits now than ever.

"You need to tell him," he said flatly. "Whether you

want to admit it or not, it's just as much his business as it is yours."

Her lips twisted. "Right. He's plagued with morning sickness just as badly as I am, has to pee every time he turns around and can't button his jeans anymore."

"That's not what I mean and you know it."

Her lashes swept down, hiding her eyes. "I appreciate what you've done here. The firewood and…and everything. But this is not your problem and it's not your business."

"Do you think you need to go it alone, just to prove to yourself that you're *competent?*"

Her chin set at that stubborn angle. "A man like you would never understand."

Give it a try.

He almost said the words. But something, some sense of self-preservation, maybe, prevented him.

He needed to remember that she was carrying another man's baby. She didn't belong in Weaver. Even her own brother talked about what a jet-setting lifestyle she'd led. And now, Derek knew she also belonged with a globe-trotting art dealer, for God's sake.

Instead, she was here. Essentially alone.

He set aside the coffee mug and stood. He went back into the kitchen and, ignoring her, pulled open a few drawers until he found an old ballpoint pen. Then he took a business card from his wallet and added a few more numbers.

He dropped the pen back in the drawer, slammed it shut and placed the card on the butcher-block countertop between them. "Since you've already proven that you won't call the Double-C if you need something like Jake asked you to, you'll have to make do with me. If you need something—*anything*—" he bit out the word "—you pick up the phone and you call. Whether it's getting you to the airport to go back to Atlanta, or getting you to town to play in Tara's shop. Understand?"

She was eyeing the card as if it were a snake.

"That baby you're carrying might be a little more important than a bruise to your ego," he added. "And if you want me to keep quiet about all this, you're going to have to face it and cooperate here."

Her gaze flew up and for a second—barely even that—before that unreadable veil came down, he could see the struggle going on inside her.

He almost wished he hadn't seen.

But she put her finger on the corner of the card and slowly slid it toward her. "Okay. I'll call."

It was a victory.

Only he wasn't sure whose war he was fighting.

Chapter Six

"Have you seen a doctor?"

Sydney sat hunched in the passenger seat of Derek's truck for the second morning on her way to Classic Charms.

After foisting his business card on her earlier, he'd left for a few hours. When he'd come back, he'd had wood in the bed of his pickup truck that he unloaded for her while she'd attempted to get her car started. By the time he was done, she was ready to admit defeat where her vehicle was concerned.

So she'd hiked up her ankle-length pencil skirt and had climbed in his truck beside him. "Yes." She watched the countryside whiz past. "To have it confirmed."

"What about now? Who are you going to see now?"

She closed her eyes for a moment. There was no point in wishing he'd drop it. That much was clear. He was like a dog with a bone. "I haven't gotten that far."

"One of my cousins is married to an obstetrician. Mallory Keegan. She practices in town."

"She's married to—"

"Ryan."

The names were slowly beginning to have order for her. Ryan was the one who the family had once believed had died. She remembered Jake talking about him because Ryan had worked for a while at J.D.'s place before she and Jake had gotten married.

But thinking about the various marital connections in Derek's family just made her wonder what had happened to end *his* connubial aspirations. Nobody but Megan had mentioned his broken engagement.

"If you don't want to see her, though, there're doctors over in Braden, too." His voice broke into her unwelcome thoughts.

"Braden?"

"Next town over. 'Bout thirty miles or so." His thumb tapped the steering wheel a few times. "Weaver's got a pretty good grapevine. If you want to keep something private for a while, Braden's a good choice."

She finally looked back at him. "You're freaking me out with this Mr. Helpful act."

"You and me both," he muttered.

He didn't add anything else, though, and she just watched him drive.

During the time he'd been gone that morning, he'd obviously showered and changed. His hair was still damp, the waves brushed straight back from his sharply defined face. She could see the collar of an oatmeal-colored shirt beneath his dark blue, crew-neck sweater and the faded jeans he'd been wearing earlier had been replaced by a fresh pair. These didn't have a tear in the knee like the others.

"Do I have hair growing out of my ear or something?"

"What?"

He looked at her. "You're staring."

She quickly looked away. "You're imagining things." From the corner of her eye, she could see his thumb drumming the steering wheel again. "A doctor in Braden might be a good idea," she said, and could have laughed at herself.

Choosing to talk about a pregnancy that she didn't want to talk about was a safer bet than getting caught staring at him?

"I'll get you a few numbers." Drum. Drum. Drum. "Unless you think you have to look 'em up yourself."

"I already know you think I'm being ridiculous. You don't have to keep pointing it out at every opportunity."

"I don't think you're ridiculous. *Or* incompetent," he added. "However, you are, without doubt, the touchiest woman I've ever met. Why is that?"

"Guess you bring out the best in me." Her voice was syrupy-sweet.

He gave her a look. "Back atcha, baby."

She folded her hands in her lap.

In addition to the wood, he'd also brought her a box of bandage strips.

She curled her fingers so she couldn't see the fresh strips covering her blisters.

But she still knew they were there.

"Before he died, my father always used to tell me I'd never be useful for anything other than my looks. Just like my mother," she said abruptly. "Turns out he was right."

He veered off the road so suddenly that she jerked against her seat belt.

He shoved the truck into park and eyed her. "Okay. I don't know what the hell kind of father you had. Talk like that's never come up between Jake and me. Your father could have been the biggest ass on the planet, but you're a grown woman now. You've got enough money to buy and sell me more times than I want to think about and you're gonna have a baby. On your own, or so you'd have me believe. What your old man used to say only matters if you let it."

"Easy for you to say," she returned. "I've *met* your parents. They're like some—" she waved her hands and shook her head "—some fairy-tale version of the perfect family. I'll bet you'd have your parents' support even if you told them you wanted to join the circus!"

"I would if they believed it was what I truly wanted. But don't make the mistake of thinking that they never called me on it when they *didn't* like what I was doing. Everyone in the Clay family has a pretty strong sense of right and wrong. As for my parents being the perfect family? They're a family," he added flatly, "because they work at being a family. Because they know that, when the day is done, it's family that counts."

"So why don't *you* have your own little family by now? Right now I wish you did, because I assume your attention would be focused on them and not me!"

His jaw flexed. "I don't know whether you need a hug or to be put over someone's knee."

She felt heat ride up her face, but it wasn't embarrassment that sent heat coursing everywhere else. "Is that a threat?"

Her question seemed to echo around the inside of the spacious truck cab. His jaw tightened and his eyes seemed to burn into her for a tense moment.

Then he looked away.

She heard him let out a long breath. When he looked back at her, his expression was neutral.

She couldn't figure out what was wrong with her that she wished for that heated intensity.

"What about your mother?" he asked more quietly.

She looked out the side window. Pressed her knuckles against it, feeling the coolness there and willing it to spread through the rest of her. "She left when I was a baby."

"Left?"

"Presumably with one of her many lovers." She gave him an uncaring smile. "At least that's the story my father gave whenever he felt inclined to talk about her." He'd trot out her lack of character, as well as the fact that she'd been willing to be bought off in the divorce settlement in favor of ever seeing her own children. And then he'd follow up with his usual condemnation—'you're just like her.'"

She didn't like the look in Derek's eyes. It was as if he were seeing right into her.

"I don't need your pity," she said flatly.

"Good. You don't have it. Your parents sucked." His gaze dropped to her midsection. "Unless you want to pass on the misery to your own child, better get over it and move on."

Exasperation soared through her. "What do you think I'm trying to do? I've left behind everything that's familiar in my life just to make a new start. A clean start! You think I want my child growing up with the kind of mother I had?" But hard on the heels of exasperation was an overwhelming tide of emotion, and her voice felt choked. "*Didn't* have?"

"Do you want this baby or not?" he demanded.

She pressed her hand against her belly. "Yes." God, yes. Becoming pregnant hadn't turned out like she'd planned, but maybe that would be her salvation.

"Look at me."

She looked at him. And put as much starch in her *"What?"* as she possibly could.

This time he didn't look amused. He didn't look annoyed. He just looked at her, his green eyes steady.

Kind.

And the tears she didn't want to shed burned behind her eyes all over again. She swallowed hard. "Don't be nice to me." Her voice felt raw. "I don't think I can take it." Animosity was so much easier. Safer.

The faint lines beside his eyes crinkled a little. "As a mother, you're going to be fine, Sydney."

She chewed the inside of her lip so hard she was in danger of leaving a hole. "Well." She cleared her throat and forced a smile. "I'm glad one of us thinks so."

He muttered a soft oath and looked away. "You're killing me here," he said gruffly. Then he put the truck in gear again, checked the road, and pulled back out onto it. "What do you want to do about a doctor?"

She realized her hands were trembling. In fact, all of her was trembling. "I'll…I'll call someone in Braden."

"Soon?"

She actually laughed. It was exasperated, but it was a laugh nevertheless. And it helped alleviate the burning behind her eyes. "Yes. *Soon.* I'm going to need to get my car fixed first."

"You can call any of the mechanics in town. There's only a few but they're all reputable. Or—"

"Unlike the handyman service I called about the furnace, you mean?"

"You called the one listed in the phone book? Able Repair?"

She nodded. "Is there another?"

"Not one that advertises itself as a handyman service,

but when you get to know people, you learn who's good at doing what. You got old Frank Able. He used to be all right when he did the work himself, but now he's more interested in keeping his new wife happy than he is with the business."

She waited a beat. "Aren't you going to tell me that I should have just called the Double-C like Jake said?"

"Guess you already know that."

She swallowed and looked away from the slanting grin that teased at his lips. "Well. I appreciate not having you remind me."

"But it does lead me to what I was going to say next. Which was, *or,* I can take a look at it later."

"You fix cars, too?"

"On occasion."

She shook her head. "I don't want to—"

"Impose?"

"Yes. Impose!"

But he was already shaking his head. "If you really intend to make a stab at living in Weaver, you're gonna have to get that word out of your vocabulary. If I didn't want to do it, I wouldn't offer."

"But that's just it! Why would you want to? I'm not your responsibility."

His thumb began beating the steering wheel again. "No. You're not. But you *are* Jake's sister."

"If you say we're *kin* again," she pointed her finger sternly at him, "I won't be responsible for what I might do."

He didn't look at her. Just checked his mirrors and sped up to pass a slower-moving car as they entered the town limits. "Kin is safer."

Her attempt at humor withered in the face of his flat tone. "I…see."

"Do you?"

She lifted her shoulder in an uncaring motion that she'd perfected when she was a teenager. "You and I wouldn't have the slightest bit in common if it weren't for Jake being married to your cousin. Our paths wouldn't have crossed in a million years. The only reason you're having anything to do with me is *because* we're—" she waved her hand "—tenuously connected through them."

"Yeah, well they did cross." He stopped at the red light. "And you can forget the high-and-mighty act. I've held your hair while you were throwing up, remember? That sort of thing's pretty much a leveler no matter how you look at it."

Her face went hot. "A gentleman wouldn't bring that up."

He gave a bark of laughter. "When did I ever claim to be a gentleman?" He drove through the intersection when the light changed. Seconds later, it seemed, he was pulling to a stop in front of Tara's shop. "And you'll have to trust me. Kin *is* safer."

She unclipped her seat belt and pushed open the door. "Safer than what?"

His gaze caught hers. And held. "Think about it."

A shiver skittered through her body and it wasn't caused by the cold air racing into the warm truck cab.

And like the coward that she was, she yanked her gaze away, slid out of the truck, and slammed the door shut. But even as she hurried carefully toward the sidewalk, she felt his intense gaze following her. Only when she was behind the safety of the shop door did she look back at the truck.

And only then did he drive away.

She pressed her hand to her chest and exhaled shakily.

"Good morning!" Tara's cheerful voice greeted her

from behind. "Come on to the back room when you're ready. I've got a whole new order of stuff we need to unpack and figure out where to place."

New start, Sydney reminded herself as she went to join Tara. And for the first time in her life, that didn't mean getting involved with a new man.

Especially a decent one like Derek.

"Got that unit ordered you requested. Bob said you can pick it up anytime."

Derek didn't look up from the blueprints spread across his desk when his secretary stopped next to him. She cleared a small spot near the corner and set a stack of folders there. "Thanks, Millie."

She didn't retreat, though, and he finally glanced up. She was wearing her coat, obviously prepared to leave for the day. "What?"

"It'd be easier for me to schedule someone else to do the install. You've got other things on your plate," she said pointedly. "You get that contract with G&G Construction and we'll all be sitting pretty for years to come."

"I'm doing the work myself," he said. "Keeps me in practice." He had no good reason for not having one of his guys put in the new unit for Sydney. But he wasn't going to examine the reasons why he insisted on doing it himself too closely. Mostly because he knew he wouldn't like what he found if he did.

"It's a small residential furnace." Millie's lined face was irritated. "You've got bigger fish to fry, dumplin'."

He sat back in his chair and looked up at her.

She'd been with CLAE since he'd bought out a local mechanical company five years ago. Then it had been called Braden Mechanical. Since then, he'd moved the office to Weaver—because it suited him—and expanded their business well beyond its roots. His latest venture was getting tied in with a huge outfit out of Minnesota. When construction was stalling all over the country, Garrett Cullum and his outfit, G&G, were still landing projects. Profitable ones.

The deal would put CLAE on the map. But Derek had to land the contract first. "Don't worry," he told Millie. "Have I ever missed a deadline before?"

She gathered up the paper wrappers from his lunch from Ruby's and tossed it in the trash. "No, but you haven't been distracted by a woman in a while, either." She pulled her gloves out of her pocket and waved them at him. "Don't think I don't know who is staying in that little cabin out by you."

"It hasn't been a secret," he countered mildly and looked back down at the blueprints for the barn that Jake wanted to build at Crossing West.

"She's working over at Tara's place," Millie went on as if Derek didn't know. "I hear she's very pretty."

"This is Weaver. In this town, sooner or later a person hears everything whether it's correct or not."

"She's not pretty?"

He didn't need Sydney inside his head any more than she already was. He'd planned to spend the day on paperwork and he'd only accomplished half of what he'd needed. "Didn't say that." He added a note to the blueprint, which was already covered in them.

Millie huffed. "Serve you right if you end up cranky and alone," she warned as she headed out of his office. "Not right. Highly educated, decent-looking young man like you not taking advantage when an available girl comes to town. It's not as if they're falling from the skies, you know," she added loudly from the other room.

She's not *available.*

He wanted to yell the truth back at Millie, but he didn't.

A moment later, he heard the front door open and close. With his secretary gone, he dropped his pencil and leaned back in the chair, pinching his eyes closed. Sydney's image might as well have been painted on the insides of his lids. Just as the feel of her slender waist was still branded on his palms.

She was pregnant. Some other guy had a claim on her already.

He dropped his hands and stared blindly at the blueprints.

Claim?

It wasn't a good word to have nagging at him. His interest in Sydney—aside from watching out for her on Jake's behalf—was as basic as it could get.

Purely physical. That was it. That was all.

It'd been three years since Renée broke it off and he'd been with plenty of women since then. Nobody who mattered beyond the moment, but it wasn't as if he'd been wallowing in celibate purgatory. He enjoyed them and vice versa. But that was as far as it went.

Sydney—if she'd *been* available—would have been no different.

He grabbed the phone from the credenza behind him and punched out a number. His cousin answered on the first ring. "Ax. Wanna hit Colbys?"

"Damn, bud. It's not even the middle of the week yet and she's got you turning to drink already?"

"She who?" The bluff was probably pointless, but he at least had to make the attempt.

"Tara had an appointment with Mallory late this afternoon. Which means your girlfriend is already closing up the shop on her own and I'm on Aidan-watch."

"She's not my—" He broke off. His cousin was yanking his chain and Derek was letting him. "I was more interested in shooting some pool than the beer. You keeping in practice?"

Axel laughed outright. "Enough in practice to clean the table before you do. When's Case getting back in town?"

"I figured he'd be back already, but I haven't talked to him yet." Their cousin, Casey, had been in Europe on some study trip. "So how *is* Tara feeling?"

"Fine."

"No, uh, no morning sickness?"

"Nooo," Axel returned, sounding suspicious. "She got over that months ago. Why?"

"No reason," he lied. "Just making conversation. You know your wife's the more interesting when it comes to the two of you."

"Yeah, I figured that out when I married her." Then Axel swore. "Gotta go. Aidan's trying to ride the dog again."

Derek hung up the phone when the line went dead. For a long moment, he eyed the blueprints and the stacks of files that Millie had left him. Then he exhaled and left it all sitting right where it was. He grabbed his coat and keys and locked up the office.

Classic Charms was only a few blocks down. Though it wasn't quite four o'clock in the afternoon, the sky was already darkening thanks to the heavy blanket of clouds that had gathered. He parked in front of the shop and went inside.

She was standing on the top of a stepladder, leaning precariously to one side as she positioned a complicated, heavy-looking candelabra on a high shelf. She looked over her shoulder at him when the opening door chimed.

The easy smile that had been on her face went completely *un*easy. "Hi." She looked back at the candelabra. Reached a little farther. Nudged a little farther.

The narrow black skirt she was wearing had a long slit up the back, revealing a mind-numbingly long leg. As well as the fact that she was standing on the toes of just one of her high-heeled black shoes on that stepladder.

Another inch and he was afraid she'd fall.

He crossed the shop in a few long steps, grabbing her around the waist. "Do you *want* to hurt yourself and that baby you're carrying?"

She gaped at him, obviously too surprised to protest when he set her on the ground. "I was doing fine!"

He yanked his gaze away from the enticing shadows beckoning below the three unfastened buttons of her silky white shirt and stepped onto the ladder. He shoved the candelabra over as far as it would go before it bumped into an ancient-looking wooden contraption next to it. "There." He stepped off the ladder and snapped it shut. "Where's this go?"

She was looking up at the shelf. "That was *not* where I was trying to position it."

He grimaced again and unfolded the stepladder. He stopped her with one hand on her shoulder and stepped up on it himself, again. "Fine. Then where?"

She crossed her arms and turned up her nose. After a solid minute of stubborn silence she finally sighed loudly. "Fine. Move it a little to the left again. And back a few inches. No, no. *Not* that far. We still need to be able to see it. Honestly, this would just be easier if I was doing it."

He looked at her. "You want me to quit?" He had no intention of letting her back up on the stepladder and she had to know it.

She rolled her eyes and propped her hands on her hips. It just gave him a better view down the front of her blouse and he glared at her because he didn't *want* to appreciate the view as much as he did.

"Bring it forward again about two inches," she said.

He nudged. He scooted. He counted to ten inside his head and he adjusted some more until finally she deemed the position of the damn thing acceptable. "I've aged a hundred years," he muttered, as he closed the ladder once again.

"I'll put it away." She reached for the stepladder, but he held it out of her reach. She exhaled noisily. "For Pete's sake. I'm pregnant, not dying."

He waited.

She threw up her hands and shook her head. "In the back room. There's a hook on the wall behind the door."

He carried the stepladder into the back room that was jam-packed with crates and cartons of every size. How the hell Tara managed to sell as much stuff as she brought in was a mystery to him, but she was obviously doing so at a busy little rate considering Axel's increasing concern that his wife was more than a little overworked.

He went back out into the main shop area. Sydney was polishing the wood counter with a cloth. Besides the two of them, the shop was empty. "Come on," he told her. "Lock up so we can go."

"It's too early yet."

"It's quarter to five."

"And we don't close until five."

He made a point of looking around them at the empty place. "It's fifteen minutes."

"It's fifteen minutes in which our customers expect us to be open."

"We. Our. You've worked here for two days."

She looked pained. "Fine. *Tara*'s customers expect her

to be open until five. And since I'm responsible for this place right now, I'm going to stick to that."

"It's going to snow any minute," he said. "There aren't going to be any folks coming in to buy an end table or one of these." Without really looking, he grabbed a fancy padded hanger off the stand next to the phone booth and waved it at her.

A hank of black, filmy fabric slithered off the hanger onto the counter between them.

She snatched the hanger out of his hand and much more gently picked up the garment. Her fingers deftly positioned two straps of black ribbon over the hanger and smoothed out the bit of fabric that held the ribbon together in a dinky excuse of a camisole.

Only when her fingers were moving over the sheer stuff did he realize he could imagine that ribbon stretching across her silky skin. Imagine taking it right back off again…

"How do you know it's going to snow?"

Snow? He suddenly felt like he was in the middle of the freaking Sahara.

She was placing the hanger back on the rack and he stomped over to the glass door, looking out. "Because it smells like it."

"I see. Is that what the weatherman said? It *smells* like snow?" She sounded amused.

He was turned on by her hanging up a damn piece of ribbon and mesh, and she was laughing at his weather prediction. If that wasn't a clue for him to get a grip, he didn't know what was.

He shoved his fists in his jacket pockets and looked at her. "My father can smell snow coming. I can smell snow coming. It's going to snow. It's going to come soon, and it's going to come heavy." His voice was flat. "So get a move on. Tara's not going to care if you close up five minutes early."

"Fifteen."

His lips tightened. "Sydney."

She stared back, just as inflexibly. "Considering how you didn't want me to let her down, I'd have thought you'd be much more interested in ensuring I follow the letter of the law exactly. Fifteen minutes isn't going to make or break a little snowfall!"

"When I said that about letting her down, I didn't know you were pregnant."

"And that changes everything? *Why?*"

"Because it does."

She crossed her arms and sat on the high stool behind the counter. "Well. I'm not going anywhere for—" she glanced at an enormous round clock hanging on one wall "—ten more minutes."

"If you want a ride," he said evenly, "you're going to get your skinny butt off that stool and—"

"Skinny!" She jumped off the stool like she'd been shot. "My butt is not skinny!"

"No. It's pretty damn perfect from what I've seen of it." Particularly the way it was outlined in that stern, sexy skirt she was wearing. "But now that you've got it moving, just keep it going toward the damn door!"

She was staring at him with shock.

But no more than the customer was, who'd just entered.

Derek eyed Tom Griffin, who was looking at them with some trepidation. "Everything all right?"

"Everything's just fine," Sydney assured him with a dazzling smile.

Fahhhn. The way she said the word lingered on Derek's nerves but he managed a nod for the balding, older man. He couldn't imagine what the guy was there for, other than to add to Derek's aggravation.

Tom gave him a wary look, but he plodded forward into the store. "You must be Tara's new assistant," he said to Sydney. "Heard she'd gotten herself one."

"I'm Sydney." Derek watched her reach across the counter and shake Tom's hand. Even from where Derek stood, he could see the red creeping up the guy's neck above the collar of his coat.

"Tom," he returned. "I, uh, I came in to pick up something for my wife. Janie."

"Of course." Sydney's blue gaze drifted past Tom's shoulder and Derek could see the "so there" in her eyes as plain as day. "Did you have something in mind or would you like to browse a bit?"

Derek wanted to bang his head against the door.

"That." Tom pointed to the outright sexy camisole that Sydney had just hung up. "She's a size eight."

"Lovely choice," Sydney said as she retrieved the hanger.

Derek managed not to groan as she rang up Tom's purchase and packaged it in a ridiculous amount of tissue paper inside a fancy paper sack with ribbon handles.

His business mercifully finished, Tom moved past Derek to the door. "Gift for the wife," he said.

Derek really and truly did not want to know what sort of underwear Tom Griffin bought for his wife, Janie. The woman taught Sunday School, for crying out loud, and Tom worked over at the tack and feed. Derek saw him at least twice a month. But he nodded. "Yeah. Got that."

He pushed open the door for the other man to leave and once the guy was gone, he looked back at Sydney. "Satisfied?"

She gave a small, superior smile. "That man just paid

one hundred and fifty dollars for that cami. Yes. I'm *quite* satisfied."

Derek nearly choked. "One-fifty!"

"It's from France."

"I don't care if it's from Mars. Who pays that much money for a few inches of ribbon?"

"A man who wants to enjoy taking it off the woman wearing it," she returned. "I've spent twice that much on panties." She waited a beat. "Well, my, my. Are you *blushing?*"

God help him. He was heating up from the inside out.

He unlocked his grinding molars. "No."

Her smile widened. But she said nothing. Merely took the cash tray out of the old-fashioned register and disappeared into the back with it. A few minutes later, she returned with her coat pulled on. She jangled the keys to the shop in front of him. "Ready?"

He shoved the door open so fast he had to catch it again just to keep the handle from crashing against the front display window. Then he moved aside and waited while she locked it tight.

"What the hell kind of panties cost three hundred bucks?"

She barely even hesitated, giving him a look through her lashes. "Think about it," she said in that smooth, Southern sway.

Then she flicked her glossy hair free of her collar and headed toward his truck that was still double-parked in the street, her crazy high-heeled black shoes snapping smartly along the pavement.

Dammit. He *was* thinking about it. Had been thinking about whatever she wore beneath her clothes from the day they'd met. Now, it was only going to be worse.

He exhaled.

Looked to the sky.

A big, fat snowflake landed right on his face.

Chapter Seven

"Oh, dear Lord. How long can this last?" Sydney was sitting on the floor of the bathroom again. Exactly where she'd been sitting every morning for the past two weeks.

Exhausted from her latest bout of morning sickness, she leaned her head back against the cool porcelain tub. "How about giving your mommy a break for a day, hmm?" She pressed her hand against her belly.

Aside from the way her waist had gotten a little thicker, her belly was still flat. She knew, because she studied it each and every day. Wondering if she started looking pregnant whether or not she'd start feeling like she knew what she was doing.

She waited a few more minutes before cautiously moving. Mercifully, her stomach stayed put as she stood and turned on the shower. While the water heated, she brushed her teeth and washed her face.

She didn't have to keep the door shut to hoard the

steam like a miser. Not since Derek had replaced the furnace last weekend. Now, if she wanted to burn a fire in the fireplace, she could do it simply because she enjoyed the coziness of it. Not because she needed it for the heat.

She pulled off the flannel nightgown that she'd bought at Shop-World when she'd finally gotten there, and left it in a heap on the rug. She still couldn't help laughing a little over the purchase. The gown was ridiculously soft but it was pink with bright green polka dots. Not exactly her usual style. She was pretty sure she hadn't worn flannel since she was an infant, and she was certain she'd never been in bright green dots.

She stepped into the shower and pulled the curtain, turning her head into the water.

She wondered what Derek would think if he knew that while she'd been perusing the store, she'd also bought herself white cotton panties that came three to a pack and cost the whopping sum of ten dollars.

Not that she had any intention of sharing that piece of information. It was bad enough that she'd taken as much pleasure in his thunderstruck expression as she had when the subject of her panties had come up between them that day at the shop.

She let the water wash over her face, but it did little to drown out that particularly sweet memory. A memory that she also knew she was holding on to longer than was wise.

What good did it do to be attracted to Derek when nothing would ever come of it?

Could ever come of it?

Just because he'd made an incredible nuisance out of himself—a useful nuisance, given the furnace and the wood and the car, since he'd fixed that, too—didn't mean that he liked her any more than he ever had. He just felt some misplaced sense of responsibility for her. Because she was Jake's sister. And because she was pregnant.

That much was perfectly clear to her.

In the scheme of things, her pregnancy took precedence over *her*.

As long as she remembered that, everything would be fine. Her pregnancy was pretty important to her, too, after all.

Which was why she needed to get a move on.

It was Friday and since she didn't have to work at the shop today, she'd made an obstetrician appointment that morning over in Braden. Derek had been adamant that he'd drive her since it had snowed yet again the day before. The fact that he had a business meeting there anyway was what made his edict a little easier to swallow. He'd drop her off at the doctor's office and pick her up afterward when he was through.

And if her stomach still felt like it was filled with butterflies—butterflies that had absolutely nothing whatsoever to do with her appointment that morning and everything to do with Derek—then she needed to get over it.

She quickly finished showering. Her hair took no time at all to dry and she dashed on enough makeup to add some color to her pale cheeks. Then she dithered over the clothes crammed into her small closet for a few minutes longer than was necessary before choosing a loose-weave ivory sweater and soft blue jeans that she tucked into her flat-heeled riding boots. She *had* bought a pair of sturdy snow boots at Shop-World, along with the nightgowns and panties, but they were for tramping through the snow.

And they were decidedly unattractive.

She looped a long brown scarf loosely around her neck and pushed several gold bangle bracelets onto her wrist before hurrying into the living room, peeking out the window to see if she could see Derek's truck yet. She didn't, so she went into the kitchen.

Even there, his mark lived on in the empty dishes that she'd been stacking on the counter for the past week. Leftovers of his leftovers, he'd told her, when he'd brought them by. Pressed on him by his well-intentioned relations who seemed to think a single man on his own didn't know how to cook for himself and needed twice as much food as he really did.

She didn't know if that was true or not, but since it meant she didn't have to attempt cooking anything much more complicated than tea and toast for herself, she'd been glad enough to take what he offered. She would have to learn how to be more self-sufficient in the kitchen before much longer. She knew that. But for now, she wasn't looking a gift horse in the mouth.

She heard the sound of his truck and the butterflies kicked into high gear.

It was ridiculous.

If there was one thing she *did* know how to do, it was socialize. In that regard, she shouldn't have any reason to feel so nervous around him. Which didn't explain why she suddenly ran back into the bathroom to take one last dash at her hair with her fingertips, to dab her favorite perfume on her wrists, to slick a hint of rosy gloss on her lower lip.

He was knocking on her door in that no-nonsense way he had when she dashed back out to the living room. She shoved her arms into her coat, grabbed her purse and forced herself to calmly open the door. "Morning."

His gaze raced from her face to her toes. "You're actually ready? On time?"

She stepped past him before pulling the door shut. "Why wouldn't I be?"

"Most women never are."

She raised an eyebrow. "I'm not most women," she returned blithely. But then she ruined her nonchalance entirely. "Wait! Your dishes." She turned on her heel and bumped right into him.

His hands caught her shoulders, steadying her. "My dishes?"

His eyes were the color of the grass at Forrest's Crossing, she thought inanely. Why hadn't she noticed that before?

"You're staring," he said.

She realized his hands were still on her shoulders. "Sorry. I was just thinking of something." Heart chugging, she hurried around him to go back inside and retrieve the dishes.

"Get a grip, Syd," she muttered to herself as she grabbed the clean items off the counter. "He's just a man. Like any other man."

She blew out a noisy breath and headed back outside again.

"Here." She pushed the dishes into his hands. "I'm going to get fat on all of those casseroles."

"You're going to get fat with baby," he corrected, looking vaguely amused. He nudged her toward the truck, juggled the dishes a little and opened the door for her.

"Not getting fat so far," she said when he came around to the driver's side after storing the dishes in the backseat. In this instance, she was happy to take his amusement over this particular point, because at least it meant he hadn't noticed anything else. Like her out-of-nowhere awkwardness where he was concerned. She pressed her hands against her belly. "I look in the mirror every morning, wondering if today will be the day that I'll see a little bump." She sighed. "Nothing so far."

"You're twelve weeks now. You haven't noticed anything?"

"Aside from all my waistbands getting a little tighter and—" She broke off, realizing what she was about to say. She shrugged instead and made a production of fastening her seat belt. "That's about it." She watched him from the corner of her eye as he turned the truck around and aimed for the highway. "What's your business about in Braden?"

Derek flexed his hands around the steering wheel. He'd noticed at least one change in her, but he would cut out his own tongue before he'd point it out. It was bad enough that he'd noticed that in the past few weeks, her full breasts had gotten even fuller. Noticing meant that he was looking, and he knew good and well he'd been looking much too closely. "I'm going over some contracts with my attorney for a job I'm bidding on in Minnesota before I go there next week to meet with them." The contract part was a flat-out lie since the G&G bid was already out the door. But not even the prospect of possibly winning the bid was enough to keep his mind off Sydney's body.

Nothing seemed able to distract him from that. Not even other women. *Available* women.

He knew, because he'd tried. He'd actually taken a woman from Braden out to dinner last weekend. And even though she'd made it more than plain that she'd have liked the evening to extend into bacon and eggs in the morning, he'd left her chastely on her doorstep the minute dinner was over.

And gone home and dreamed about Sydney.

He unclenched his death grip on the steering wheel. "You talked to your brother lately? They coming home soon?" He hoped so. The sooner Jake knew about her pregnancy, the sooner Derek could hand off watching after her.

"I already know they won't be back for another few weeks. But I haven't spoken to Jake in a few days." Sydney unwittingly dashed that hope. "I talked with my aunt Susan yesterday, though. She said they're all doing fine. Jake's boys haven't gotten themselves expelled from any schools lately."

Derek knew that Jake's twin sons were nothing if not mischievous and had—more than once—been invited by the school they were attending to please attend somewhere else. "I suppose you must have met their mom? Jake's first wife?"

She nodded. "I knew Tiffany, of course. But we were never particularly close." She shifted in her seat, pulling open the lapels of her coat as if she were too warm. "Tiffany was always more interested in the fact that he was a Forrest than she was in Jake personally."

He turned down the heater a notch and kept his gaze trained resolutely out the front windshield. He hadn't failed to notice that she was wearing a beige sweater that faithfully clung to her body, starting at her long neck and heading down. Not even the scarf draped loosely around her neck did any sort of job of disguising the lush, jutting thrust of her breasts.

"Talk to anyone else?" Even to him, his voice sounded rough and he felt the glance she gave him.

"Charlotte. She's still in Germany. Will be for a while, it sounds like. She's made no secret that she thinks I've lost my mind for moving to Weaver, if for no other reason than that I like to shop too much." She laughed a little. "I told her she hasn't seen Tara's shop yet, or she'd realize I don't have to go as far as she thinks to find some pretty fabulous treasures."

Like hundred-and-fifty-dollar underwear?

He turned down the heater yet another notch. "Anyone else?"

"No." Her gaze slid his way. "Are you trying to get at something specific?"

They'd reached the highway and he gave it some gas. "*Him*. Have you told *him* about the baby?"

She made a soft sound. "We're back to that again?"

"Have you?"

"I have not spoken with Antoine." Her voice had gone tight and she folded her arms around her waist, which only succeeded in plumping up her breasts even more.

He turned the heater as low as it would go without actually turning it off. "Why not?"

"Because he hasn't called me," she said slowly, as if he wouldn't understand otherwise.

"I thought you were a modern woman. Your fingers work to dial a phone, too, don't they?"

She held out her hands, slender fingers spread, and made a point of looking at them. She wore a narrow, diamond band around her thumb. "Guess they would, if I wanted them to." She curled her fists again and tucked them around her waist. "Instead of beating that particular dead horse, why don't we talk about *your* love life for once?" She gave him a sideways look and smiled sweetly. "Or don't you have one anymore since your fiancée broke it off?"

He should have known that she'd hear about that sooner or later. It was common knowledge. But the fact that his love life was presently deader than a doornail, unless he counted his way-too-disruptive dreams, had nothing to do with Renée. "That was a long time ago," he dismissed.

"And we're not talking about love lives. We're talking about you telling the man that you made a baby with that he's going to be a father."

"Maybe you need reminding that contributing sperm doesn't a father make." She looked out the side window.

"It does in my family."

"Well not everyone is like your family, are they?"

That was true enough, he figured. And after that, they said no more until they reached Braden. He found the medical complex easily and parked in the busy parking lot. He knew if he tried to go in with her that she'd protest, so he just waited while she undid her seat belt and fastened up her coat again. Then she flipped down the sun visor and looked in the little mirror there, dabbing more glossy stuff on her lower lip and running her fingers through her gleaming hair, tucking it behind her ear.

The diamond stud in her earlobe seemed to wink in the morning light.

He knew she was dawdling.

He just didn't know why.

"Are you nervous?"

"What?" She gave him a quick look and flipped the visor up with a snap. "Of course not." As if to prove it, she smiled—tightly, in his opinion. "What time do you expect to be finished with your attorney?"

He blamed his slow-wittedness on that earlobe. Not the diamond that was a surprisingly modest size for someone of her means, but the lobe itself. He'd never noticed before what a sexy thing that little curve of flesh could be. Right there…the long line of her neck so close…her nape.

He cleared his throat. Business meeting, he reminded himself. "'Bout an hour or so. Shouldn't be any longer than you'll be."

"Fine." The look she gave him was vaguely suspicious.

Or maybe that was just his guilty conscience, since he had no meeting scheduled at all. He'd only used the excuse because she would have refused the ride if he hadn't.

"Don't rush on my account," she told him as she pushed open the truck door. "I'll wait for you in the lobby if I don't see your truck out here."

He nodded. "That works." She still seemed to be hesitating. "Unless you want me to go in there with you, after all."

Her shiny lips parted and her gaze shied away. She shook her head quickly. "What about your meeting?"

"I can reschedule."

"I can't decide if that's sweet or intrusive." But she shook her head again, more determinedly this time. "Regardless, thank you. But it's not necessary at all. It's more than enough that you drove. I'll see you when you're done." She slid out of the truck and quickly slammed the door.

Derek waited until she disappeared inside the building before he pulled out of the parking slot. He'd find a coffee shop or drive around town for the next hour, if he had to. He'd only be circling the small town about a hundred times.

"Everything's looking fine, Sydney. And don't worry about not showing yet. You will be soon enough." Dr. Fleming, the OB/GYN, held out his hand for Sydney's to help her sit up from where she'd been lying on his examining table. "Any nausea? Dizziness?"

The paper gown she was wearing rustled as she arranged it over her legs. "Not dizzy unless I'm nauseous," she said wryly.

He didn't even glance at her above the chart that his nurse handed him. "Often?"

"Most every morning."

"Hmm." He clicked his pen and made a note on the chart.

She realized she was chewing her lip. "Is that normal?"

"It's not abnormal," he said, which Sydney didn't think told her anything. "Get dressed and we'll meet in my office to go over some paperwork," he added briskly as he handed off the chart to the nurse and let himself out of the small room.

Sydney eyed the nurse. "Is he, um, always so…brief?"

The girl didn't seem offended by the question. "Dr. Fleming has a pretty busy schedule," she said. "He's a popular doctor."

Since the man—aside from his abrupt bedside manner—was ridiculously handsome, Sydney didn't doubt that. In fact, he was exactly the type of man she'd always gone for. Tall, dark, impeccably groomed and seemingly lacking in any sort of warmth. "Is he a *good* doctor?"

"Oh. Of course." The nurse gave a reassuring smile. "He's very well qualified. And of course he has privileges at the Weaver Hospital, so you shouldn't have any worries there. He'll go over all of this with you in his office, but even if he doesn't make it to the hospital for your delivery, you'll be well taken care of, anyway. The staff there is wonderful." She closed the chart and tucked the end of her stethoscope in the lapel pocket of her pink scrubs. "I delivered all three of my babies there." She reached for the door. "Take your time dressing. I'll show you to Dr. Fleming's office when you're ready."

Sydney waited until she was alone before hopping off the exam table and pulling off the paper gown. It was ridiculous to be wishing that she'd taken Derek up on his offer to accompany her inside. It's not as if he would have been in the examining room with her.

Would knowing that he was sitting in the waiting room have made her feel more relaxed?

Or would it just have underscored the fact that he was *not* the father of her baby? That the father of her baby—a man who could have been Dr. Fleming's double—would never be around?

The truth was, she didn't want Antoine around. He didn't want to be there, and she didn't care.

And what kind of a person did that make her?

There was a small mirror on the wall above the hook holding her clothes, but she didn't look at her reflection as she finished dressing. What was the point?

The woman looking back at her looked just like the woman who'd given birth to her. She hadn't cared, either.

As promised, the nurse was waiting when Sydney opened the door, and she showed her into a comfortably furnished office. Sydney sat down in one of the cushioned chairs placed in front of the wide desk and waited for Dr. Fleming.

The obstetrician that she'd seen back home had had a half-dozen framed photographs on the credenza behind his desk, all featuring his wife and children.

The credenza behind Dr. Fleming's desk was bare of everything, including dust.

The same soft, classical music that had been piped into the waiting room was piped into the doctor's office. She supposed it was meant to be soothing, but after about ten minutes of it, it grated on her nerves.

She got out of the chair. Glanced out the office door down the empty hallway. She could hear the chatter of nurses, but not the deeper tone of the doctor's voice. She glanced out the large window beside the desk and chairs.

They were on the second floor and the window overlooked the parking lot.

She spotted Derek's pickup truck immediately.

And just that easily, her edginess seemed to fade.

She gathered up her coat and purse and left the office, stopping at the desk at the end of the hallway that sported a discreet "billing" sign. She paid for the office visit and when the girl there wanted to schedule Sydney's next appointment, told her that she wouldn't be back.

The other woman's eyebrows went up a little. "It's important that you receive regular medical care."

"I agree." She tucked her credit card back in her wallet. "It's just sinking in that I should be getting that in Weaver."

Then, feeling better having made what seemed a momentous decision, she left the office and took the elevator down to the first floor, pulling on her coat as she went.

She knew the moment that Derek spotted her exiting the building, because he immediately pulled out of his parking space and drove up to the entrance. She quickly climbed up beside him.

"Everything go okay?"

She nodded. "Perfectly."

"When do you come back for your next appointment?"

"I don't." She looked at him. "I've decided to go to your cousin's wife instead."

He was obviously surprised. "Why?"

"Because she practices in Weaver where I live," she said simply.

He seemed to absorb that. "Fair enough." Then he put the truck in gear. "It's lunchtime. You want to stop somewhere to eat or head straight back?"

"Let's stop." She was suddenly feeling famished. "Somewhere I can get a hamburger the size of your fist."

He fisted his hand, seeming to measure it. "Suds-n-Grill it is, then." Then his eyes narrowed. "You sure you're okay?"

"Yup." She eyed his profile as he drove out of the parking lot. As usual, he needed a shave. But not even the blur of stubble was enough to detract from the sharp edge of his jaw. If anything, she was beginning to realize it was only enhanced. "What's your office like?"

He gave her a curious look. "I don't know. It's an office. Desks. Chairs. Stacks of files everywhere, despite the salary I pay my secretary, Millie. Why?"

"Do you have a credenza behind your desk?"

Curious turned downright quizzical. "Nothing behind my desk except a chair and an old chest I swiped from the attic at the Double-C. Why?"

She just shrugged and smiled to herself. She'd bet her last credit card that he had a picture or two of his family on that chest. "No reason. So tell me about the Suds-n-Grill. Is it far?"

He grinned crookedly. "Only three turns away last time I checked."

Chapter Eight

Two days later, Sydney stared at Derek's truck and shook her head. "This is so completely unnecessary. If I wanted a truck, I'd buy one."

Derek was standing beside her just outside the cabin door. He'd come to pick her up for another Sunday dinner. The sun was shining again, brighter than ever, and for once there wasn't any breeze to speak of.

All in all, it would be a particularly lovely Sunday, if not for the stubbornness of the man beside her, who'd just blithely announced that he expected her to use his truck while he was away.

"Buy all the trucks you want," he said smoothly. "God knows you can afford 'em. But until then, you've got this one to use."

"It's *your* truck. I don't want to take your truck."

"You're not *taking* it. You're using it to get around while I'm in Minnesota. No big deal."

"But I don't want to im—" She broke off when he gave her a look. "Listen. I realize that my car isn't the best choice given the snow. But it's been running fine since you worked on it. I doubt it'll leave me stranded between here and town. The roads are always plowed and that's the only place I'll be going."

"Humor me."

"Derek—"

"Sydney," he drawled in return.

She huffed, exasperated. "Fine. But consider it fair warning when I tell you I'm not good with large vehicles."

"It's not a tank, for God's sake. It's just a dually."

She eyed the vehicle parked in front of the cabin. In comparison to her two-seater, the truck was massive, from its big crew cab to its dual wheels. "I backed a truck through a paddock fence once, and it wasn't as big as that." She waved her hand toward it.

"I ran a tractor over a motorcycle once," he countered. "Things happen."

Her jaw dropped. "You did? When?"

His arms were folded lazily over his chest. "When I was ten. Pissed off my dad pretty good, because I wasn't supposed to be on the tractor in the first place." He smiled faintly as if he were fond of the memory. "Grounded me for the entire summer."

"I was seventeen and my father gave me that," she gestured toward the little car parked inside the shed, "after I destroyed the fence."

"A reward?"

She shook her head. "It might seem that way. What it really was, though, was one more reminder of how much like my mother I was. It had been her car, originally."

"You're not like your mother." He headed across the snow. "Come on. Afternoon's wasting and we've got

Sunday dinner waiting. My sister's cooking this time and she does a mean pot roast."

Everyone seemed to take it for granted that Sydney would be interested in another dinner with his family.

Which she was, but that didn't mean she intended to give in where her car was concerned. She pushed her hands in the pockets of her coat and tore her eyes from the way his well-worn jeans fit his backside as she followed him. "You don't know anything of the sort about me and my mother. You never knew her."

He pulled open the truck door and his scratched leather jacket parted, revealing the way his dark blue T-shirt hugged his wide chest. "Did you?"

She yanked her gaze back to the truck again. "I told you she left when I was a baby. No. I didn't know her."

"So you're just taking your old man's word for it."

"I look just like her." She still had that worn snapshot she'd taken so long ago from her father's desk.

"If you want to find reasons to be like a woman you say you don't want to be like, knock yourself out." He gestured toward the truck interior. "You can drive to Sarah's. You might as well get behind the wheel of this thing and get accustomed to it. I might be loaning it to you while I'm gone, but that doesn't mean I won't care if you do hit something."

"You can't force me to drive your truck. Not today and not this week while you're gone."

He lifted an eyebrow. "I think that's debatable," he said mildly. "But you're going to need to get used to driving something larger than that toy of yours sooner or later."

"Why?" She propped her hands on her hips. "Because *you* say so?"

"Because a car seat isn't going to fit. They face backward and aren't even supposed to be in the front seat."

Her building indignation fizzled and her throat tightened.

He was right. Of course, he was right. A car seat would never fit into her two-seater. "You know a lot about car seats."

"Lot of babies being born in the family these days and I've been known to babysit a time or two." He gestured again. "Now, you going to get in, or do I put you in?"

It was all too easy remembering how comfortable he'd looked holding that toddler at the Double-C.

She stepped past him and placed her foot on the running board to pull herself up. "You wouldn't put me in," she scoffed lightly. It was better than dwelling on how ill-prepared she was for becoming a mother, everything-about-pregnancy book or not. And certainly safer than dwelling on *him*.

"Put my hands around your hips for a few seconds? Why the hell would I want to do that?" His voice was wry. "Now move it."

Butterflies skittered around in her belly. She looked down at him. He hadn't moved away from where he stood; she was slightly above him. "You could care less about my hips," she countered. "What you do care about is the baby. You've made that abundantly clear."

His gaze captured hers. "Might not want to test that theory, cupcake. You're a beautiful woman. And I'm just a man."

Her heart seemed to jerk toward her throat. She was rapidly learning that there was nothing "just" about Derek.

"A stubborn man," she corrected, more breathlessly than she would have liked. But she would have said anything then to break the spell he seemed to be casting over her.

A new start. She had to remember that. A man-free new start. Antoine hadn't wanted her, with a baby. Derek was only interested because of the baby.

She wasn't so…infatuated with the man that she would allow herself to forget that fact.

She pulled herself the rest of the way into the truck.

"Stubborn recognizes stubborn." He closed the door and rounded the truck, climbing into the passenger seat.

"I'm not stubborn."

He snorted. "Right." He snapped his safety belt into place. "And the Pope's not Catholic." He handed her the keys. "Start 'er up."

She pushed the key into the ignition. The truck smoothly started with a deep, growling purr. "I'm a very easygoing person!"

He leaned closer and gave an exaggerated sniff. "No drinking and driving. No drinking, period, when you're pregnant."

He was so close she could smell the fresh scent of soap he used. "Trying a little stand-up comedy? Don't quit your day job."

The corner of his lips kicked up. Her stomach dipped and swayed and she knew she couldn't blame it at all on morning sickness.

"Try reverse."

She swallowed hard, willing her hormones back onto their usual dusty shelf and focused on the task at hand. She pulled the seat forward and moved the mirrors until she could see in them, then put the truck in reverse and cautiously inched away from the cabin, following the ruts in the snowy gravel. "I feel like I'm driving a semi."

"Everything's relative."

"I'm sure this thing isn't exactly fuel-conservative."

"And your toy car is?"

He had a point, though she'd choke before admitting it.

"This thing'll run on alternative fuel, too," he added dryly, "so don't worry too much about being green. Now pull yourself around and try not to hit the logs that line the drive."

She hadn't even known there were logs lining the drive, thanks to the snow covering everything. She turned the wheel, backing into a circle. "I'll never be able to park this thing in town."

"You can park behind the shop. There's a wide alleyway there that you can drive straight through if you need to."

She sighed noisily and changed gears. She pressed the gas a little harder and the engine growled. "You're one of those people who has an answer for everything, I suppose."

His lips twisted. "A few graduate degrees does that." Then he tapped the gear shaft. "You're in neutral, honey. Try again."

She could feel her face getting hot as she braked and made the adjustment. She couldn't help wondering how many degrees he did have. She only had one, and barely one at that. She'd been more interested in parties than studying and she'd graduated by the skin of her teeth. "I warned you."

"Relax." His voice went gentle and his hand covered hers on the steering wheel. He squeezed her clenched fingers. "It's just a truck."

"It's a weapon in the wrong hands," she muttered, trying not to dwell on the warmth of his palm. She flexed her fingers, loosening her death grip. His hand left hers and she pulled in a deep breath, driving slowly toward the highway. "How, um… How long are you going to be in Minnesota?"

"I leave tomorrow, early, and come back Thursday night." His voice turned dry again. "Try not to miss me too much."

"Don't you worry none," she returned with all the Southern sweetness she could gather. "I'll enjoy the peace." But she *would* miss him and she knew it. Which meant it was just as well that he'd be gone for a little while. She came to Wyoming to find some independence, not be taken care of by someone, no matter how irritatingly well-intentioned he was trying to be.

"Well, while you're enjoying the peace, call Antoine. Tell him you're pregnant. It's the right thing to do."

Her hands went tight again around the steering wheel. "And it's also not your concern."

"Why'd you break up?"

"He was sleeping with his assistant!" Strangely, she was less embarrassed by the admission than she should have been. "Satisfied? Can we drop it now?"

"He's an ass," he said with plain disgust. "How long were you together?"

Longer than they ever should have been. She shot him a look. "Why don't we talk about *your* ex-lovers instead of mine?"

He just waited.

When it came to lasting one out, he'd win hands down. She sighed again. "Two years," she said. But Derek wasn't the only one who could be persistent. "Why'd your ex-fiancée break it off?"

"Because she wasn't in love with me." His voice was matter-of-fact.

Then *she* was an ass, Sydney thought, but mercifully managed to keep the thought to herself. "How long ago?"

"Three years."

She flexed her fingers around the steering wheel wondering how far he'd let her push. "Megan says you're still pining for her. Is that true?"

"Megan's a kid. She doesn't know anything."

"That doesn't answer the question."

"Imagine that."

If he hadn't still had feelings for Renée, he'd have just said so. Which meant he *was* still pining.

The thought tasted sour. She turned onto the highway and picked up speed. The truck handled with surprising ease. "Where is she now?"

"Megan? At home, I would imagine, since her mom is cooking."

She gave him a look. "I meant your ex-fiancée."

"You don't say."

She exhaled, aggravated more than she wanted to admit. Possibly because she knew she was becoming too curious about his personal life. It wasn't just the principle of returning his nosiness. It was an intense interest in his answers. "Why is it that you feel perfectly free to bug me about *my* life, but put up the stone wall when I return the favor?"

"You're digging into the past. It's pointless. That baby you're carrying is the future. Not pointless."

"Exactly." She pounced on the thought. "*My* future. Not Antoine's."

His lips thinned. "If he doesn't know, then you're assuming a helluva lot."

"Oh, for heaven's sake! I'm not assuming anything," she exclaimed. "He doesn't want children. I knew that when we started seeing each other. Nothing's changed." Nothing except Sydney.

"You'll never know unless you tell him." He practically bit off the words. "The turnoff for Sarah's place is right up there."

She was exasperated with him, but he looked positively livid. "I thought she and Max lived in town," she said tentatively.

"It's a back way."

She slowed and made the turn and followed the road for several minutes before he pointed out a few more turns and they arrived at a two-story house with several cars parked in front. Her head felt congested with screaming thoughts as she pulled up behind another truck—obviously from the Double-C considering the brand that was painted on the door.

"Nothing's changed," she repeated. She put the truck in park, turned off the engine, and handed him the keys. "I know, because I *did* tell him."

Then, before he could comment further, she got out of the truck and headed toward the house.

He caught up to her, though, before she could even lift her hand to knock on the door. His hand circled her upper arm and turned her around to face him. His face was grim. "You told him. When?"

She deliberately lifted her arm out of his hold. "You are truly the nosiest person I've ever met. But if you must know, I told him when I found out I was pregnant." She smartly rapped her knuckles on the door. "He said no thanks and that's the end of that story."

She heard him swear beneath his breath. "I'm sorry."

She lifted a shoulder. "What for? You're not the one who dumped me and my child." It was amazing how little emotion she felt saying that. If anything, she was relieved to be out of her old life.

The door swung open to reveal Megan's smiling face. "I bet Eli that you'd come together," she said in a greeting.

Derek tried dragging his attention away from Sydney to his niece and failed.

"What were the stakes?" she was asking Megan.

His niece grinned even more broadly. "He has to do my chores for two weeks." She led the way into the house.

Sydney's laughter was soft as they followed.

Derek felt like he'd been hit with a sledgehammer, and *she* was laughing with his niece.

He grabbed Sydney's arm, hauling her into the study that was off the main hall.

She gave him a startled look. "What's wrong now?"

He managed not to slam the door when he shut it. "Why the *hell* didn't you tell me this two weeks ago?"

Her eyebrows rose. She looked down her superior, tilted-up nose at him. "Because it wasn't your business then, any more than it is now."

His hands fisted. "You made it my business when you asked me to keep your little secret." He raked his gaze over her slender waist. She was wearing a button-down white shirt that hugged her curves right down to the shirt-tail hem that she'd left untucked over the hips of her dark blue jeans. She still managed to make the simple clothes look fancy.

She propped her hands on her hips, and the gold bracelets around her narrow wrists jangled. "Only because you were sticking your nose in where it doesn't belong," she reminded him. "If you hadn't barged in on me like you did, you wouldn't even know!"

"Is that what you really want? For nobody to know? Maybe you *don't* want the baby." His hands closed around her shoulders, forcing her to look up at him. "Maybe my finding out just got in the way of your plans."

She was staring at him like he'd lost his mind. "Derek." Her voice was soft. "You're hurting me."

He froze. His fingers were digging deeply into Sydney's arms. Maybe he *was* losing his mind.

He swore under his breath and released her. "I'm sorry." He turned away, prowling around his brother-in-law's study. He shoved his hands through his hair. "Go on and find the others." His voice was gruff. "I'll be there in a while." After he got himself in hand. Stopped acting like a lunatic.

She moved, but not through the door. Instead, she walked across the room, not stopping until she was standing right in front of him. A frown was pulling her dark brows together. "Are you all right?"

Obviously not. He'd never hurt a woman in his life. Not even Renée. "You ought to be telling me to go to hell."

"*Now* you'd listen?" The corners of her lips twitched upward. Her blue eyes were dark. Soft. "What's really going on here, Derek?"

Life had been so much simpler before he'd gone to the cabin that first time. She'd opened the door and looked down that sexy nose of hers at him and he'd been in knots ever since.

He rubbed his hand down his face. He couldn't go around blaming her for something Renée had done. "Nothing I want to get into," he muttered.

"Too late for that, I'm afraid." She stayed right where she was. "You know my worst secret. So…?"

"Being pregnant isn't a *worst*."

"It is when you do it deliberately."

He stared. She couldn't have shocked him more if she'd tried. "You got pregnant on purpose?"

She gave a faint, humorless smile, and shook her head,

finally turning away, giving him enough space that he could breathe in without feeling like he was inhaling her.

"I don't know if that's even true," she admitted after a moment. "But I'm thirty-one years old. I know the facts of life. Antoine and I worked because we both wanted the same things. No children. No commitment. But the years started to pass. I got older. He got…more attractive." She gave him a squinty look. "Not fair how that happens," she added. "Women get wrinkles and look old. Men get wrinkles and look distinguished."

"If you think you're looking old, you need glasses. You're beautiful and you know it."

Her lips twisted. "The only thing I know is that even after I knew he was involved with his adolescent assistant, I still slept with him. Made certain of it, in fact. Our sex life had been in the toilet for months and I knew I wasn't in love with him. But I…didn't like my position being… usurped. Certainly not by someone a decade younger than me." She sat on the rolled arm of a leather chair. "So…I seduced him. Is that *worst* enough now?"

"Renée was pregnant," he said abruptly. "When she broke it off, she knew she was pregnant."

Sydney's lips rounded in a silent O.

"She never told me," he added. "I found out a few months ago. I ran into her in Cheyenne at her father's funeral."

"She had the child with her?"

"She never had the baby." He was determined to let it out, once and for all. Maybe then he could get over the strange hold Sydney's pregnancy had on him. "She had an abortion."

"Oh, Derek." Sydney pushed off the chair and came over to him again, wrapping her arms around him before he even had a chance to move away. "I'm so sorry."

Her head was tucked beneath his chin. Her dark hair smelled like vanilla.

"No wonder you've been so insistent about me telling Antoine," she said softly.

He closed his eyes, trying not to dwell on the fingers she stroked down the back of his head or the soft push of her breasts against him, but it was no good. He'd gone as hard as a green teenager the second she'd touched him.

"Sydney—" He broke off, not even sure of what he wanted to say. *Take off your clothes and lay back on Max's wide, wide desk?*

She pulled her head back, peering up at him. "Yes?"

It was the last thing he wanted to do. But he deliberately set her aside and turned away from her. "If Antoine came to you now and said he wanted you back, would you go?"

"No," she said quietly. "I didn't like the person I'd become. I was exactly what my father had told me I'd be. And I don't want my child to have that person as a mother."

He looked back to see her looking down. Her palms were pressed flat against her abdomen. "This is a new start for us both," she finished, then looked up at him and smiled.

It was like taking a blow to his gut. And he knew that if they stayed in there alone for one more minute, he *was* going to put his hands on her and damn the consequences.

He strode past her and pulled open the door. "Come on. Food's waiting and you're eating for two."

She followed him, but stopped short of leaving the room as she gave him a quizzical look. "If you'd have known—if she'd have told you she was pregnant. What would you have done?"

"Been a father." His voice was flat.

Her blue gaze seemed to drill into him for an eternity. "You'd have been a good one," she finally said. Then she stepped past him and headed down the hall toward the voices and laughter they could hear.

He let out a long breath. And after a few minutes, he followed.

"Come on, Sydney. Put some back into it."

Sydney eyed Derek. The only thing separating them was a good fifty feet of snow-covered ground. "Put some back into it," she muttered. "What does he think I've been doing?" She held out her gloved hand toward Megan.

The girl grinned and dropped a well-packed snowball into Sydney's hand. "You can do it," she said under her breath.

Sydney wasn't so sure. Her efforts at hitting Derek with a snowball littered the snowy expanse fronting Sarah and Max's house, all having fallen embarrassingly short. "I don't know why I let you and Eli talk me into this," she told Megan. It had been the kids' idea to have a snowball fight after they'd finished dinner.

"'Cause it's fun and you still *owe* him," Megan reminded. "Eli shoved snow down my collar once and I had to pummel him."

"You tried," Eli called.

"I do owe him," Sydney agreed. Though knowing what she now knew about what motivated the man tended to lessen the urge for revenge.

"Right." Megan was nodding enthusiastically. Then she dropped her voice. "Aim for Eli. I'll get Derek."

"You can try, Meggie." Derek had a grin on his face.

The first one since he'd dropped his bombshell in the study about Renée, and Sydney for one was glad to see it.

He tossed the snowball he was holding from one hand

to the other. Evidently, maybe in honor of the threatening gray sky, he was wearing gloves for once. “Never hurts to try.” Beside him, Eli was fairly falling over his feet from laughing. “Even when you fail.”

“Children, children!” Derek’s mother appeared in the doorway of the house, laughter in her voice. “Get in here and have your apple pie while it’s still warm. We’re all waiting for you!”

Derek held out his arms and dropped the snowball. “Saved by the food bag, cupcake.”

Sydney narrowed her eyes and focused on his dark blond head. She wound her arm back and with everything she had, let the snowball fly.

It sailed past his head, only narrowly missing him because he suddenly ducked.

“I *knew* you could do it,” Megan crowed and launched her own volley at her brother, hitting him on the shoulder. Eli didn’t waste any time firing back, and Sydney laughed as she darted out of range, heading toward the house.

She pointed her finger at Derek. “Next time you call me cupcake, I won’t miss,” she warned.

“Next time don’t throw like a cupcake.” He reached the door before she did and pulled it open. Megan and Eli darted around them, racing after each other into the house. “Cupcake.”

Sydney stopped short and glared up at him.

But the glare didn’t hold any water.

Not with the way her heart was pounding and her mouth was suddenly running dry.

“Dammit. I knew this was going to be a problem.”

Her lips seemed to tingle beneath the green gaze he’d focused on them. “What?”

His jaw canted for a moment. The edge of his teeth showed. “This,” he muttered.

Then his gloved hand went behind her neck and his head dipped, his mouth covering hers.

Her mind went white. Brilliant, snowy white.

And just when her stunned senses began to notice details—like the tantalizing rasp of his shadowed jaw beneath her smooth gloves, the way his lips seemed to carry the taste of the wine he'd drunk with dinner, and the pulse of her heart beating between them—he was lifting his head again.

She sucked in a deep breath, grateful for the way the cold air streamed inside her lungs, freezing out the intense heat threatening to boil her from the inside out. "Oh, my," she breathed as she exhaled.

"Yeah."

"We, um, we can't let that happen again." Despite the cold air, her cheeks still felt hot. "It'll just get in the way of…of—"

"Everything?"

"Right." She ignored his ironic tone. "I mean, I'm having a baby!" Her voice had risen and she looked around guiltily, hoping that her words hadn't carried.

"I'm aware."

"And you, you're still getting over Renée."

"I was over her years ago."

"Then getting over what she did," she amended.

That, at least, he didn't deny.

"I'm sure you don't want to be a substitute for Antoine, and I am no substitute for Renée."

"Did you want a substitute for him? From what you've said the jerk sounds worse than an ass."

"No, I don't want a substitute!" She gave him a quick look. "But you did. That's why you've been on me like a wet blanket since you found out I was pregnant."

"Sydney, if I'd been on you the way I wanted, we'd both be in sex comas."

Heat streaked through her all over again, not at all mitigated by knowing he was more concerned with the baby she carried than he was with her.

"Now get inside before someone comes looking for us again."

"I don't care for apple pie."

"Fine. We'll stay out here." He waited a beat. "Better yet, I'll take you home."

Her hormones were on fire. She wasn't sure how a sex coma would feel, but she could make a good guess. And a better guess that finding out with him would pave her new start with complications the size of boulders.

"Pie," she said almost desperately.

"Smart choice."

"Now I know why I was never good at making them," she said under her breath. "It sucks."

He gave a bark of laughter and dropped his arm over her shoulders. He pressed a kiss to her forehead that—despite its brevity managed to make her feel unsteady—and then nudged her inside. "Yeah. It does suck."

Chapter Nine

"When does Derek get back in town?"

Sydney didn't look up at Tara from the necklaces she was arranging on a cloth-covered board. "Tonight." She had to work at sounding nonchalant. "I think," she added for good measure. She held up a particularly lovely necklace that was made of a deceptively simple set of twisted wires. "Have you taken classes or something?" She looked over at Tara, who was sitting behind the old-fashioned register making out a deposit for the day's sales. "This one is remarkable."

"Thanks." Tara glanced at the necklace. "And I've mostly taught myself. Easy to do when you love doing it." She finished counting out bills, made a notation on her deposit slip, and sat back, arching her back. "I will be so glad when this baby comes." She blew out a breath and awkwardly scooted off the stool. She rubbed her hand over her pregnant belly that was draped with an oversize flannel shirt. "Would you mind taking the deposit to the bank?"

"Of course not." Sydney put the necklace back in place and slid the board beneath the glass display case. She intended to buy the necklace as a birthday gift for Charlotte and wondered if Tara could make a coordinating bracelet. "Just go sit and put up your feet for a while. I'll take care of closing when I get back."

"Think I will." Tara still had her ever-present smile on her face, but it was a little less cheerful than usual as she plopped down into an antique wing chair they'd brought in the day before.

Sydney pulled on her coat and dropped the deposit bag in her purse, then took the cordless phone over to Tara and left it on the small end table next to the chair. "I won't be long."

Tara just waved her off. "This is Weaver. Nothing takes too long."

The bank branch was within walking distance, which saved Sydney from having to take Derek's truck from where she'd parked it in the alley behind the shop. Even though it hadn't snowed once since he'd left town and she could have easily used her own little car, she'd still driven his truck.

She couldn't quite explain it. He'd expected her to drive it, so she had. Because she hadn't wanted to disappoint him? Or because she was simply being practical? Becoming more comfortable in a larger vehicle since she'd have to deal with that soon enough because of the baby?

She wanted to think that was the only reason, but was afraid it wasn't.

She reached the bank and went inside. There were lines at both teller windows and she joined the shorter one, taking her place behind a heavyset woman with bright red sausage curls circling her head. The woman looked Sydney up and down, smiled, and turned right around. "You're Derek's new girl."

Was he so present in her mind that even complete strangers picked up on it? She looked at the woman. "Excuse me?"

"Derek Clay." The red curls bobbed up and down. "Heard he'd finally taken up with someone new. You're working for our dear Tara, isn't that right?"

"I do work for Tara," Sydney agreed slowly.

The other woman beamed. "I heard about you from my neighbor. Millie Greenfield. She's Derek's secretary. I'm Dolores Wells. My friends call me Dori."

"Right, Dori, and you're holding up the line." A wizened old man had taken his place in line behind Sydney. He gave Sydney a polite nod.

"Quit your complaining, Howard," Dori returned without heat and moved up to the teller's window.

"Woman's a gossip," Howard whispered loudly to Sydney.

"No worse 'n you," Dori chimed from the window.

Howard harrumphed and glared at Dori's generous backside. "If the woman'd start living her own life, she wouldn't have to yammer on about ever' one else's."

Dori turned smartly on her fuzzy-lined snow boots and sashayed back to Howard. She tucked a wad of cash in her sensible black handbag. "Start living a life with you, you mean?" She sniffed. "I'm a decent woman, Howard Grimes. You want me to live with you, you'd darn well better put a ring on my finger first!" Then she looked at Sydney. "That's something I wish you young girls would learn, too."

Sydney was still blinking when Dori strode out of the bank.

"Marry her." Howard harrumphed again. "We're too old to be thinkin' such nonsense." He transferred his glare from the door Dori had exited through to Sydney. "You just gonna stand there holding up the line, or get your business done?"

"Sorry. Guess I haven't been called a young girl in a while." She hurried to the window and handed over the shop's deposit. Soon she had the receipt in hand, and she left the window, slowing as she passed Howard. "I don't think there's an age limit on marriage." She smiled. "And if there is, there shouldn't be."

"Achh." Howard waved his hand. "You *are* too young to know nuthin'." Then he pointed his gnarled finger in her face. "Just don't go messing with that Clay young'un. He had enough of that with that spoiled brat from Cheyenne."

If Howard only knew. "I don't plan on messing with anyone, Mr. Grimes."

"Call me Howard," he said, heading toward the window. "Ever'one does."

Smiling to herself, Sydney left the bank. Her gaze wandered along the street as she walked back to the shop. All of the sidewalks had been shoveled clear of snow and every storefront seemed ridiculously picturesque.

She couldn't wait to see Weaver in the summer.

Tara was still sitting where Sydney had left her in the shop when she got back. "That was entertaining," she said as she put the receipt in the cash drawer. "Howard Grimes wants to live with Dori Wells, but she's not having anything to do with him unless he marries her first."

Tara grinned. "And aren't you fitting in nicely where the Weaver grapevine is concerned."

Sydney pulled out the necklace display again and set it on top of the counter. "I like to think so." The thought was immeasurably cheerful. She held up the piece she wanted for Charlotte. "Can you make a bracelet to match?"

Tara shrugged and nodded. "Sure."

"Excellent. My sister will love them." She set the necklace aside and rearranged the remaining ones. "Honestly, Tara, I know about a dozen people who'd love these." She looked over her shoulder. "In fact, I know a jewelry dealer who'd love to get her hands on your designs."

Tara looked intrigued, but she still shook her head. "Between taking care of my family and the shop, I barely have the time to make enough jewelry to keep the shop stocked."

"But if you had the time?"

Tara tilted her head against the back of the chair. "Well, gosh. If I *had* the time, I'd just as soon rock my husband's babies and make jewelry all the time. Forget about the shop." Then she smiled impishly. "Don't let Axel hear that, though. He'd be all over it like a wet blanket."

Which only made Sydney think of Derek all over again. She tried to ignore the jitters inside her. She wasn't a kid. The days of getting nervous just from thinking about a boy were supposed to be long past. "I assumed you wanted to keep the shop open."

"I do." Tara looked around the stylishly eclectic interior. "My mother always wanted a shop of her own." Her smile turned reflective. "When the opportunity came for me to open here, it was like I was finally giving her something she'd never had while she'd been alive." Her gaze went back to Sydney. "And I do love this place. But it's not my life's goal." Her hand circled over her belly. "Not anymore."

"Well." Sydney leaned back against the counter. "What would it take for you to have more time to pursue rocking those babies and making jewelry all the time? More employees, maybe?"

"A partner," Tara said simply.

"I could be your partner." The suggestion came without a plan. But as soon as the impulsive words were out, she knew she meant them. More than she'd meant many things. "Weaver's my home now. I know I still have a ton to learn, but I've got the money and the willingness to try."

Tara lifted an eyebrow. "Yes, I imagine you do. But then we'd just be two pregnant ladies running this place, wouldn't we?"

Sydney's lips parted but she couldn't summon a word to save her life. She realized she was pressing her palm over her still-flat stomach and cleared her throat. "I'm not even showing. Did Derek tell you?" She could hardly believe it of him, but he wouldn't be the first man to live down to her expectations.

She'd just let herself believe he was different.

Never a good thing where Sydney was concerned. Her judgment in men had always been faulty, even well before Antoine.

Tara's lips were pursed in a silent whistle. "No," she said after a moment. "But hormones recognize hormones and I took a shot. I wasn't entirely certain until now." She lowered her feet to the floor and sat forward. "What's Derek's…involvement?"

"He's not the father," Sydney said quickly. "He just, uh, found out. I haven't told my family yet. I've been waiting for them to get back from California next week."

"I see."

Sydney doubted it. "And I know I should have told you when you offered me the job. I wasn't honest with you and

I won't blame you at all if you don't take the partnership idea seriously."

Tara waved a dismissive hand. "Please. You're not the only one who's ever had reason to keep a thing or two to herself." Her lips twitched. "I looked a lot more pregnant than you by the time I told Axel he was going to be a daddy for the first time." She relaxed again into the chair. "But that's a story for another day. So, prospective partner, what sort of changes would you want to see at Classic Charms?"

Excitement and relief rolled through her, leaving her slightly light-headed. "You're actually considering this? Not...not because you feel sorry for the unwed pregnant lady or anything?"

"Should I feel sorry for you?"

"No! I just... This seems too easy."

"Easy doesn't always have to be bad," Tara pointed out humorously. "I managed to learn that. I figure you can, too. So, is this something you really want to pursue?"

"Yes," she said with certainty. "Absolutely. I can buy in at fifty percent if you want. Or...or less...if you don't want a full partnership."

"Fifty percent sounds good to me. And better to have you as a whole partner than chance you opening up your own shop across the way."

Wholly bemused, Sydney sank down onto a rough pine cocktail table positioned near Tara's chair. "I could never do that," she assured her. "And I don't think there should be any changes here. Why fix what's not broken? No, strike that. *One* change."

"Oh?"

She leaned over and plucked a necklace off the display board. She dangled it in the air between them. "You need to let me introduce you to my jeweler friend."

Tara's eyes narrowed. Then she smiled again, more broadly than ever. "Deal."

"You did *what?*" Derek stared at Sydney, obviously shocked. It was later that evening and he'd stopped by her cabin on his way home from the airport in Cheyenne.

Sydney had expected to surprise him. But she hadn't expected him to be horrified. "You heard me. I'm going into partnership with Tara at the shop."

"But why?"

She pushed off the couch and faced him. He hadn't even noticed that it was a *new* couch. One she'd bought from the shop and had delivered the day before. He also hadn't noticed the new television that was now affixed above the fireplace or the large area rug that lay on the gleaming wood plank floor that had previously been hidden beneath the ancient, worn wall-to-wall carpet. "Why *not?*"

"You're pregnant," he reminded.

"So is she!"

"That's different."

She gaped. "Why?"

He grimaced. "I don't know! It just is."

She crossed her arms. "Admit it. You don't think I'll be a good partner to her."

"I didn't say that."

"You didn't have to. But it's obviously what you think!"

"God help me," he muttered. "If you really knew what I was thinking—" He broke off and shoved his hands through his hair, leaving the dark blond strands standing on end. Then his gaze focused on hers like green lasers. "And even if I did think it was a bad idea—" his hand flew up "—which I don't," he emphasized, "you shouldn't let that stop you from doing something you believe in."

Her defensiveness fizzled. "I don't understand you at all."

"I want you to start believing in yourself," he said flatly. "And stop jumping to the worst conclusions at every damn turn."

Her back stiffened again. "It's not much of a jump when you—" she waved her own hand "—react like you are. *You did what?*" she mimicked his horrified tone. "What else am I supposed to think?"

"I was surprised," he said. "You never do what I expect."

She still wasn't sure that was such a great thing. "And what did you expect?"

"That you'd get tired of Weaver!"

Defensiveness was so much easier to take than the disappointment that swept through her. "I see." She turned away. "Well, you might notice that I'm making myself quite at home here." Her throat was tight as she retrieved his truck keys from where she'd left them on her kitchen counter. She held them out to him. "Get used to it."

"I noticed. I noticed everything."

Everything that was visible, perhaps. But what about what wasn't?

She lifted her chin. "I am *going* into partnership with Tara. We're going to meet with an attorney to work out the details as soon as we can set it up."

"But she's had the shop on her own for years."

There was an ominous burning behind her eyes and since he wouldn't take the keys, she dropped them on the ancient army-green footlocker that she'd kept as a coffee table simply because she liked its worn charm. If she didn't get him out of there soon, she was going to humiliate herself. "I guess my waving the Forrest money in front of her worked its usual seductive magic," she drawled.

"Don't."

She lifted her eyebrows, silently inquiring.

"Don't put on the snob hat, Sydney. It doesn't fit you anymore."

She turned on her heel and went into the kitchen, swiping her fingers beneath her lashes.

She heard him swear behind her, and then his hands caught her shoulders, turning her toward him. "Don't cry." His voice was gruff. "Yell at me or throw a dish at me or do something, but don't do that."

"Well I'm so very sorry," she snapped, even as the dreadful tears started sliding down her cheeks. "Heaven knows the last thing I want to do is make *you* uncomfortable."

His gaze looked toward the ceiling. He shook his head, then looked back down at her. "Honey, I've been uncomfortable since the first day we met."

She inhaled sharply, stung.

But the sting dissipated when he caught her chin between his fingers and lifted her mouth to his.

And then she just inhaled.

Him.

When he finally straightened, she was pathetically grateful to see he was as breathless as she. He pushed her to arm's distance, staring down at her. "If you want me to go, say so now," he warned. His voice was low. Rough.

And it thrilled her beyond measure.

"I don't want you to go," she whispered. Not now. She was very much afraid, not ever.

His eyes closed for a minute, his thumbs roving over the points of her shoulders. Then he hauled in a deep breath. Let it out slowly and finally opened his eyes. His gaze burned over her face as warmly as if they were his hands. "You make me forget what control is."

Her heart jerked. She sucked in her lower lip and unsteadily stepped closer to him, despite his hold on her shoulders. If he'd really wanted to keep her at bay, he could, but he didn't, and she took courage from it. "Not with me." She wanted to know that he was as out of his element as she. Wanted to know that she wasn't alone in the desire she was drowning in.

"You're pregnant."

"And healthy and normal." She slipped her hands around his neck, linking her fingers behind his head. "So unless that turns you off—"

"Not likely," he interrupted, and found her mouth with his again. His arms slid around her back, his hands gliding over her rear, pulling her up to her toes against him. "Are you wearing hundred-and-fifty-dollar panties?"

Her lips vibrated from his words and she laughed softly. "The three-dollar variety, I'm afraid. I can change them if you want—" Her words ended in a squeak when he lifted her right up off her feet and carried her into the bedroom.

"All I want is you out of them."

There was something to be said for straightforward bluntness. Especially when it was spoken in his low, husky voice. It made everything inside her shiver with the sort of amazed delight she hadn't felt since she'd had her very first kiss so long ago.

He set her on her feet at the foot of the bed and tugged her blouse off her arms. He tossed it aside only to pull her back to him as if he begrudged even that brief separation. "Every time I've closed my eyes I've imagined this." His fingers played down her spine, deftly disposing of her bra along the way. "Every...single...time."

"And to that I say stop imagining." She tugged at the hem of his sweater until he yanked it off and then she went on her toes, fitting her curves even more tightly against him. "And start doing."

She felt his fingers between them as he pulled down her zipper. "You're sure?"

"I'm sure I'm going to have to cause you serious pain if you don't stop asking me." She was also going to melt into a boiling puddle and disappear into steam if she didn't feel the weight of him on top of her, and quick. She yanked at his belt, her fingers clumsy in their haste. "I don't think you know what pregnancy hormones can do to a woman," she warned, not exactly joking.

He gave a muffled laugh, though, and caught her hands, drawing them away, to finish the job himself. And with satisfying quickness, she suddenly found herself flat on her back with his broad shoulders blocking out the light from the living room beyond him.

And then humor went quiet.

They both went still.

Sydney's heart was pounding in her ears, threatening to deafen her to everything. But she could feel his pulse, too. And feel the deep breath he drew in the push of his wide chest against her breasts.

She slowly arched up until her lips grazed his. "I'm glad I came to Weaver," she whispered.

In answer, he opened his mouth over hers. And she opened her body to his. And everything that she thought she'd ever known about making love was blown to bits in the exquisite pleasure that engulfed her.

Later…much later…Sydney stared up at the ceiling, her mind as adrift as her body.

"Sex coma," Derek murmured beside her.

She inhaled slowly. Exhaled even more slowly. She felt lax right down to her soul.

She couldn't recall ever feeling so loved.

Not *loved.*

She sat bolt upright as the term sank into her consciousness.

"What's wrong?" He'd pushed himself up on his elbow and was looking at her.

She dragged her gaze away from his disheveled hair and shadowed jaw only to get caught on the allure of his naked backside. She'd left a trail of kisses all the way down that sexy spine of his. Kissed the dimple just above his butt. And he'd laughed and flipped her over, returning the favor until neither one of them had been laughing.

Again.

No. Definitely *not* loved. That wasn't what was going on between her and Derek. This was just sex. Pure and simple sex. Mind-boggling, world-shattering sex.

But still…just…sex.

"Nothing," she said hurriedly. "Um…gotta pee." Oh, that was sheer brilliance. She scooted off the bed and raced into the bathroom, slamming the door shut.

But for once, she didn't have to pee.

She closed the lid on the commode and sank down on it, burying her face in her hands. *Hormones. They're out of whack, and that's all this is. Pure sex. Pure hormones.*

She'd never fallen in love with any man in her past. Derek was no different. He couldn't be different. He *wasn't* different.

She repeated the assurance several times until she thought maybe it had sunk into her head. Then, afraid that Derek's habit of barging in on her might still be alive and well, she flushed the toilet and washed her hands at the sink.

Her reflection in the mirror stared back at her.

Her hair was a mess. Her cheeks were rosy from Derek's whiskers. Her lips were red and swollen.

She looked wholly loved.

And Derek *wasn't* like any other man she'd ever known.

Her shoulders drooped and she closed her eyes.

Sydney, Sydney, Sydney. Have you learned nothing?

"You okay in there?"

At least this time, he'd knocked.

She cleared her throat, feeling a sudden urge to either laugh hysterically or cry—or both—and turned off the water. "Yes."

The bathroom door opened and Derek stood there, just as naked as she. His gaze drifted downward from her face then back up and despite what they'd just done, her breath went short all over again.

"Look at you," he murmured.

She wasn't interested in looking at herself. It was all she could do not to stare too noticeably at him. She made some sort of unintelligible sound and started to pull the bath towel off the hook, intending to wrap it around herself.

"Wait." His hand stopped hers and just that easily, the warmth inside her spread. Turned liquid all over again, as if she weren't still recovering from some major ecstasy.

"Derek—" She broke off when he suddenly kneeled in front of her, his hands coming up to cover her belly. Her head swam.

"I thought you said you weren't showing."

His words barely penetrated the fog engulfing her. "What?"

His thumbs slowly brushed back and forth against her skin. "You're showing," he said. His hair brushed against the inside of her wrist when he leaned forward and pressed his mouth against her navel.

Her knees turned to gelatin. Without thought, her hands clutched his head. "I…am?"

"Yeah." His head moved. His mouth drifted over her hip. Kissed his way down her flank. His hand drifted, too, downward, slowly downward, and finally slipped between her thighs.

She couldn't help the moan that escaped when his fingers found her. "Derek—"

"You are the sexiest woman I have ever met." He nudged and she suddenly felt the cold porcelain sink against her backside. But that was the only thing cold. The rest of her was turning white-hot beneath his touch.

"You're just saying that—" her head suddenly felt too heavy to hold up and she let it fall back "—to be polite."

His soft laughter tickled her thigh. "Oh, yeah. I'm always saying that sort of *polite* thing to the good women of Weaver, whenever I run into 'em at church."

A giggle rose in her, which was ridiculous, considering the wicked torment of his teasing fingers. "I'm going to just get bigger."

"You're ripe," he countered, running his lips upward again. "That's one of the sexiest things. Here." He kissed the decidedly evident bulge in her abdomen. "And here." He went higher still, and caught the tight bead of an aching nipple between his lips.

She pulled in a hissing breath, pure sensation going like a current from his lips to her core.

"And here," he murmured, his fingers sliding through her moisture, gliding, rubbing.

Her legs trembled and she instinctively arched against him. He made a low sound in his throat, a purely masculine growl of pleasure. "That's it, cupcake."

She laughed breathlessly even as pleasure was ripping through her, and sank her hands into his hair, giving a good, sturdy yank. "I'm not a cupcake!"

"Maybe I forgot to tell you." His mouth moved to her other breast while his fingers delved and swirled and wound the coil inside her ever tighter. "They're my favorite dessert." And then those teasing fingers turned marauder and slid straight to the heart of her.

She gasped, the coil inside her close to snapping. But not even then did he stop. He came off his knees and lifted her against him and she wound her legs around his hips, and tightened them around him as he sank into her.

Sensation exploded inside her.

"Hang on."

She couldn't do anything but, as he carried her, filling her to the limits of her sanity, back to the bed and lowered her slowly, deliberately, onto the center of it, and then moved against her until she was crying out his name. And only then did he give that low growl again, and as she shattered into a million bits of light, she could feel him shattering right along with her.

When she finally woke, sunlight was streaming through the window and the bed beside her was empty.

The realization took a moment—too long of a moment—to sink in.

He'd left.

She didn't know why she hadn't expected that.

She grabbed the other pillow and held it to her face. Surely it was her imagination that told her she could smell him on her pillow. An hour or two in her bed wasn't a night. Or a lifetime.

She exhaled, throwing the pillow aside. She was not

going to lie there and dwell on what wasn't. She and Derek had made love. More than once.

But that didn't mean anything had changed. No matter how much chemistry there was between them, he still couldn't think of her pregnancy without thinking of the child he wasn't given the chance to have, and Sydney knew enough to realize that she could never be satisfied with just being a stand-in for Renée. She would never, ever, let her child feel like a replacement for the one Derek had lost.

That much she was certain of.

So she shoved aside the tangled sheets and climbed out of bed. It was only as she was halfway through her shower that she realized she didn't feel the least bit of morning sickness.

In fact, she was ravenous.

She finished her shower and pulled on a pair of jeans, marveling at how—seemingly overnight—she couldn't get the zipper up even halfway. She exchanged them for a pair of brilliant blue velour sweatpants and matching hoodie. She had enough staples in her refrigerator and kitchen cabinets now that she could easily make her own breakfast, but the pecan-studded cinnamon rolls at Ruby's Café seemed much more appealing than oatmeal. And there would be other people there. People to distract her from the one person she needed to get out of her thoughts.

So she put on her boots and cap and coat and grabbed her purse and headed outside.

Only then did she hear the distinctive *thwap* of a log being split.

And only then did she realize that the white truck with the Double-C logo on the door that he'd arrived in the night before was still parked next to his truck that she'd been driving all week.

And if he'd left, at least one of those trucks would have been gone.

Her nerves jangled.

Feeling embarrassingly shaky all of a sudden, she carefully stepped through the snow, rounding the back of the cabin.

And there he was.

Hatless as usual, the thick waves of his hair tumbling over his forehead. Not even wearing a coat, just the same heavy toast-colored sweater that she'd dragged off his shoulders the night before. He rhythmically set a log, then swung the ax, sending neat pieces of firewood tumbling to the ground.

But as much relief that she felt coursing through her at the sight of him, she felt an equal measure of shock at the sight of the man standing beside him.

"Antoine," she said, bringing both men's attention around to her. "What on *earth* are you doing here?"

Chapter Ten

Antoine Kristoff was just as tall as Derek. He wore a black cashmere coat and leather gloves over his knife-edged trousers. His dark hair was slicked back from his patrician features and his brown eyes were full of annoyance.

Derek's clear green gaze, on the other hand, was completely unreadable, his breath a cloud in the clear morning light as he turned toward her. If she'd had any doubts whether he already knew the identity of their visitor, they evaporated.

"We have a few things to discuss," Antoine said. "In private."

She didn't want to discuss anything with him, in private or not. "Why didn't you just call? How'd you even get here?" There were no other vehicles around aside from hers and Derek's.

Antoine's perfectly shaped lips thinned. He never had

liked his actions being questioned. "This is more important than a mere phone call, Sydney Anne." He gave Derek a dismissive look that annoyed her down to her bones.

Derek propped the end of his ax on the chopping block. Only a matter of hours ago, she'd been practically screaming his name while he groaned and emptied himself inside her, but now, his eyebrow peaked as he gave her a steady look. "Maybe you better talk to the man, Sydney Anne."

All of the nausea that she hadn't felt upon waking came home to roost. She dragged her gaze from Derek to Antoine. "I'll talk to you inside," she told him. "I'll be there in a minute."

He pulled back the cuff of his coat, none too subtly reminding her just how valuable his time was.

Sydney couldn't have cared less. She was much more interested in Derek than whatever had brought Antoine to Weaver. She waited until he'd disappeared around the side of the cabin.

"I thought you'd left," she told Derek.

"Were you expecting him?"

"What?" Shock yanked her voice up several notches. "Of course not!"

His eyes narrowed slightly as if he were deciding whether or not to believe her.

She closed the distance between them. "If I'd known he was coming, I would have convinced him not to," she said more quietly. "Derek—" She shook her head, wishing she knew what to say to convince him. "He's *nothing* to me."

"He is to that baby you're carrying."

The fact that he was right didn't make the words any more palatable. "That sort of thing matters to men like you," she said huskily. "Not to men like Antoine."

His lips twisted and he looked down at his ax, yanking the blade out of the stump. “Yeah, well, he’s here now, isn’t he? So I guess you’d better go inside with him.”

She chewed her lip and didn’t move. “Derek—” His gaze slanted over her and despite everything, her heart climbed up into her throat. “I’m glad you didn’t leave.”

He grabbed another log and balanced it on the stump, then swung the ax down onto it, cleaving it in two. “Guess that makes one of us.”

She winced.

Decent man or not, he knew how to cut her to the quick and she couldn’t even summon a defense.

She turned away and heard him mutter an oath. “Sydney.”

She didn’t look back at him. “What?”

“Are you going to be all right?”

Her eyes burned. Of all times to realize she’d fallen in love with him. But the knowledge was suddenly just there. Crystal clear and undeniable.

She managed a nod, though she wasn’t certain of any such thing, and went inside.

As much as she didn’t want to have anything to do with Antoine, it hurt less going into the cabin with him than it would have to stay outside where Derek clearly didn’t want her.

Antoine was standing in the middle of the living room, studying the Solieres. “Hanging them in this hovel is a sacrilege,” he said as soon as she entered. “They belong in a museum or a secure gallery at the very least.”

She closed the door behind her with more force than necessary, and dropped her outerwear on the couch. “Your gallery, I suppose?”

He gave her an “obviously” look. “Everyone we know

thinks you've taken leave of your senses moving out here the way you did. It's entirely embarrassing."

"I can't imagine why. But thank you so much for asking how I am, Antoine. Always nice to know how concerned you are. How is Trina?"

"She quit." He reached out and plucked one of the paintings off the wall. "Went to work for Sotheby's."

"I'm surprised she gave up on you so quickly." Maybe Trina was smarter than Sydney had given her credit for. "How *did* you get here?"

"I drove a rental up from the airport in Cheyenne." He looked more disgusted than ever. "This place was barely on the GPS. Plus I had to park down by the highway and walk the rest of the way or chance losing an axle. This trash heap is hardly your usual style, Sydney Anne." He lifted the painting. Tilted it slightly, studying it from different angles.

"It's not a hovel. Nor is it a trash heap. It's a hundred-year-old cabin, and I'd think you'd at least have some respect for *that*." She grabbed the painting and pulled it out of his hands. "What are you looking at?"

His lips thinned so much they nearly disappeared. "The two Solieres I sold to Geoffrey Reyes while we were in Antibes," he said. "You remember them?"

She hung the painting back on the wall. She wasn't likely to forget Antibes even though she wanted to. "I remember."

"They were forgeries."

Well and truly stunned, she turned around and sat on the couch. "You're kidding."

"I wish I were," he muttered. He yanked off his coat and folded it over his arm. Sydney wondered if he was afraid it would get hovel cooties if he set it down somewhere.

"Well." She propped her feet on the footlocker and folded her hands over her lap. "My Solieres have been authenticated several times." They'd had to be, in order to get them insured. "I'm not worried they're forgeries." Though she could well imagine the hot water Antoine had gotten himself into with Reyes. The eccentric billionaire had a notoriously hot temper.

"I know." His eyes stayed on them where they were hanging above her head. "I want them."

She put her feet back on the floor. Sat forward. "I beg your pardon?"

"I want them," he repeated, as if she were dim. "If I give them to Reyes, he'll…refrain from making a stink about our little mix-up."

The collector had paid millions for the paintings. The publicity would be more than just a "stink" over a "little mix-up." It would put into question every art deal in which Antoine had ever been involved.

She frowned. "Did you *know* they were forgeries?"

"Don't be stupid." He looked more annoyed than ever, more likely because of the fact that he, too, had been duped, than that Sydney had held any such suspicion about him. "Not that I can convince Reyes of that." He gestured toward the paintings. "That's why I need them."

"Well, I'm not selling them," she said, amazed that he would think that she would now, when she'd always refused to do so before. It was because of the Solieres that he'd even sought her out in the first place.

"I don't want to buy them," he said dismissively. "I want them. And you're going to give them to me."

Her eyebrows shot up. "Uh…don't think so."

"This is all your fault," he said.

At that, she could only gape. "*I* didn't convince Geoffrey Reyes to buy forgeries. You did that all on your lonesome." Albeit with a little help from the nubile Trina, who'd seemed as busy charming Reyes as she'd been her boss.

"I mean if you hadn't run off on me the way you had, I could have already gotten the paintings to Reyes and everything would be fine."

"Run off?" She pushed to her feet. "You're the one who showed me the door," she reminded him. And thank God he had, because who knew how long it would have taken for her to come to her senses otherwise. "Now, when you're up to your neck in hot water, I'm suddenly *not* too old and *not* too pregnant for you?"

He made a face, his gaze dropping to her midsection. "If you'd gotten rid of it like I asked you to do, I wouldn't even be here now. How much bigger are you going to get, anyway?"

Irritation rapidly passed annoyance on the way to pure rage. She was thrilled with her little baby bump, but he made it sound as if she were as big as a house. "Feel free to think there is no baby anymore," she said flatly. "Because there isn't. Not one that you will ever be involved with."

"Yes, well, that would have been fine. Except now things have changed."

And then it dawned on her.

"Oh, my God. How stupid am I? What are you going to do? Threaten me for custody of a baby you don't even want if I don't give you my Solieres?"

"Not entirely stupid," he said.

For a long moment, she could only stare. What on God's green earth had she ever seen in him? "You're despicable."

He was clearly unmoved. "I'm practical. Just how badly do you want to raise your little heir in peace?"

He touched the edge of the middle painting, adjusting it slightly. "A few paintings seem a reasonable trade."

"How do we know you won't come back for more?"

Neither one of them had noticed the door quietly open, or that Derek was standing there. And he'd obviously heard.

Sydney wanted the floor to open up and swallow her whole. Now he'd know just the sort of pond scum she used to associate with.

But Derek wasn't even looking at her.

Instead, he was eyeing Antoine with the coldest expression she'd ever seen on a person's face. "How many more paintings?" he went on, stepping soundlessly into the room. "Or more money? Or whatever *thing* happens to be of value to you at that moment?"

Antoine glared at Sydney. "Who is this person?"

"I'm the man she's going to marry," Derek said before Sydney could even get out an introduction.

Her legs went numb. She sat down with an inelegant plop.

Antoine's thunderstruck eyes looked from Sydney to Derek and back again. "I don't believe it."

Neither did Sydney. But she couldn't seem to find her tongue to save her soul.

"Believe it." Derek advanced far enough into the room that Antoine actually took a cautious step back. It was a smart move on the other man's part, because Derek was about a hairsbreadth from planting his fist in the man's pretty-boy face. He didn't look at Sydney, who was staring at him, her eyes so huge they looked like blue bruises against her pale cheeks. "So what's our assurance that this is a one-time deal?"

Whether or not Antoine was intimidated by him, the

jerk obviously came to the conclusion that Derek was a man set on making a deal.

"I'll waive my rights as its parent."

Its.

Derek had to deliberately relax his fists. "You'll legally sign away all of your paternal rights to Sydney's baby?"

"The second she hands over the Solieres."

"Done." Sydney spoke up then, rising to her feet. She was still pale, and she didn't look at Derek, but she was clearly determined. "I'll have my attorney draw up papers by Monday. You can have the Solieres the second they're signed."

"Monday! You really have lost your mind. I can't wait until Monday." He fished in his folded coat and pulled out a sheet of paper. "I figured this would be the offer, and I've come prepared. My attorney prepared this release." He waved it at her.

She shook her head. "I wouldn't touch anything your attorney prepared with a ten-foot pole. *My* attorney. Monday. Take it or leave it."

"Well, look who finally got a spine," Antoine spat and Derek could practically see steam coming out of his ears.

"That's right," Sydney said, her voice low and furious. "I've found my spine. And I've got Forrest money bracing it up even more." She rounded the footlocker, her finger nearly jabbing into Antoine's face. "So help me God, if I ever see your face again after this little deal is done, I will make sure your career is over more surely than Geoffrey Reyes ever could."

Antoine actually stumbled back a foot. "Christ, Sydney Anne. Pregnancy is making you bitchier than ever."

Her teeth bared, she said, "Get. Out."

"When will I meet you?"

"We'll be in touch," Derek said, adding a helping hand in shoving the man toward the door.

"You don't know how to reach me."

"Not too many rented Escalades in Weaver," he assured him flatly. "Don't you worry your pretty face about how we'll find you." He shoved the man out the door and slammed it shut behind them.

Antoine took a hasty step forward, catching himself from landing face-first on the ground. He shook out his coat and eyed Derek. "Trust Sydney Anne to fall on her feet. She always did. Of course it's obviously gotten harder for her now that she's past her prime considering how she's lowered her standards in someone like you."

"You know," Derek said, conversationally, "I don't give a damn what you think of me. But you keep insulting Sydney and I'm going to have a real problem with that. You're in my neck of the woods now, Tony. Don't mess with me. Don't mess with my family." His fist shot out and even though Antoine flinched as if he fully expected the blow that Derek badly wanted to deliver, he merely latched his grip around the man's silver necktie.

Then he hauled him close until they were practically nose to nose. "This is wild country," he said softly. "Dangerous country. *Clay* country. And if you want to know what that is, you just say the name when you get back to town." He tightened his grip a little more, until Antoine coughed a little, gasping for air. "We understand each other?"

"You're welcome to her," Antoine muttered, yanking back. He smoothed down his tie with a hand that Derek was satisfied to see wasn't exactly steady. "I would've been done with her long ago except for all those pretty zeros in her bank account."

“That’s it,” Derek said, shaking his head. And he planted his fist in Antoine’s perfectly shaped nose.

The man stumbled back, swearing at Derek. “You’re freaking crazy.”

Derek stepped toward him again. “No,” he said. “I’m a man of my word and I warned you. You want another lesson?”

Blood was seeping out from behind the hand Antoine had cupped over his face. Proving that he had some sense, he raised his other hand, staving Derek off. “No. I’m going.” He headed over the snowy ground toward the gravel drive, his fine leather shoes slipping and sliding as he went.

Derek didn’t budge until Antoine was out of sight.

Only then did he go inside the cabin.

Sydney was huddled on the couch, her clasped hands pressed to her mouth.

“He’s gone.” Derek closed the door behind him. His knuckles were stinging like hell but he didn’t look at them to see if they were bleeding, too. Sydney’s eyes were still wide and shell-shocked and she wasn’t saying a word. He nodded toward the paintings hanging on the wall behind her. “How much are they actually worth?”

She finally lowered her hands. “The three together? Seventy-eight point six million.”

Jesus.

He actually felt the need to sit.

“And you have ’em just hanging here on the walls of this place, where anyone and their mother’s brother could break in with nothing more complicated than a swift kick to the door?”

“This is my home,” she said huskily. “Where else would I have them?”

“A bank vault?” He shoved his hands through his hair.

He'd known the Forrests had money. Big money. He just had never thought too far down the road about *how* big. Thanks to the success of the Double-C, the Clays as a rule were a comfortable lot. Collectively, pretty much one of the wealthiest families in the state. But they didn't go around dropping megamillions on ugly art that they blithely hung on cabin walls. "I need a drink," he muttered.

"It's ten o'clock in the morning."

"No kidding." He exhaled and sank down on the couch.

"You didn't have to tell him that," she said after a moment.

"What?" Seventy-eight point six million. The number kept swirling in his head.

"That you were marrying me. I know you were just trying to be helpful. To protect me."

A woman who'd blithely hang seventy-eight point six million dollars' worth of art on her walls needed protection. But despite his stunned bemusement, he had the good sense not to make that particular point. "That baby needs a father," he said instead.

Her face grew pinched, and he wondered if he'd have been better off with a different argument. "You mean *you* want the chance to be a father. Any available pregnant woman would do."

"It's not any available pregnant woman I'm willing to marry. It's you."

"*Willing* to marry." Later, when she was alone, Sydney would let the pain of that wording leech through her. For now, she built a dam against it and instead let the lingering outrage over Antoine's "deal" carry over to Derek. "Well, bless your heart," she said with as much Georgia sweetness as she could muster. "That's just the sweetest thing." She pushed to her feet. "I'm afraid I'll have to decline."

"Cut the crap, Syd."

She propped her hands on her hips. "What do you want me to do? Fall to my knees in gratitude that you're *willing* to marry me? If I wanted a husband who was merely *willing,* don't you think I could have found one by now? It certainly would have been easy enough. Since I've been out of training bras there've been plenty of fawning idiots around who'd have been happy to put up with me in exchange for the pleasure of getting a fingertip on my little corner of the Forco legacy."

"*Little* isn't a word I'd use to describe that sort of thing." He waved his hand at the paintings. "And I don't give a damn about the Forco legacy, except to wish right now that it didn't exist."

"Well, it does," she said stiffly. "And I don't ever intend to marry anyone unless he can see *me* without seeing *it.* Now, if you don't mind, I need to find a lawyer somewhere around here who can write enough legalese to keep Antoine at bay for the rest of our lives." Her gaze drifted to the Solieres. Parting with them made her ache. But knowing Antoine would be gone forever was worth the loss.

"My cousin's married to a lawyer."

She felt a sudden urge to laugh, though she felt no humor whatsoever. "Another cousin. I should have known."

"He's in Sheridan. I'll drive you there today."

Being cooped up in his truck with him for any length of time wasn't a good idea. "There's no one here in town?"

"No one as good as Brody. You want the best, don't you?"

He knew she did.

So that settled that.

And an hour later, she was sitting beside him in his truck as they made the trip to Sheridan. Several hours later, they were driving back again. She had the thick document in her hand, along with Brody's instructions to have it signed in front of unimpeachable witnesses.

It was dark when Derek pulled up in front of her cabin.

They'd hardly said two words directly to each other the entire time they'd been on the road.

"Your other truck is gone," she said inanely.

"Dad sent one of the hands over for it."

"Ah." She nodded, and the awkward silence started to swell again. She could hardly bear it. "Thank you for the ride," she said. "And for arranging things with Brody."

He nodded.

She should have been getting out of the truck and going inside. But instead, she hesitated, chewing the inside of her lip. "I never had a chance to ask you how your trip to Minnesota went."

"Fine." He shifted restlessly. "Good. We got the bid. The jobs will keep us busy through at least the next few years."

And that was the only point of true pleasure she'd felt since Antoine had slithered his way to her door. "Congratulations. I know what a big deal that will be for your company."

He nodded.

She didn't know why she was still hesitating. She forced her hand to unclip her safety belt. "Good night, Derek."

"I've always seen *you,* Sydney."

She went still. The dam sprang a leak. She grabbed his hand and pressed it to her belly where, even through her cashmere coat, they now could feel the swell of her child. “You’ve seen this,” she corrected. “We both know it’s true. If we pretend otherwise we’re just lying to ourselves.”

“Maybe that’s how it started.” His voice seemed to come from some deep, cavernous place. “But that’s not *all* there is,” he reminded pointedly.

“Yes,” she managed calmly, which just proved that even when your heart was breaking, a Forrest could still keep up a good front. “You’re an amazing lover. But I didn’t come to Weaver to find a lover. I came to Weaver to make a new life.”

“And you’re doing that. What’s to stop you from marrying me?”

The dam sprang another leak. And another, and another, and there weren’t enough thumbs in the world to plug them all. “Maybe the fact that you never asked me? Maybe the fact that I’ve never wanted to be married before? Particularly to someone who’s not even in *love* with me? I’m exhausted,” she added abruptly, and pushed open the truck door. “I’m going to bed. Alone,” she added before he could think otherwise.

“We’ll talk in the morning,” he said behind her.

She shut the truck door on him and kept walking.

Fortunately, her feet knew the path to her front door by heart because tears were clouding her vision. She unlocked the door, went inside, and locked it after her.

Only then did she hear his truck drive away.

Chapter Eleven

When Derek called Sydney the next morning, she didn't answer.

When he drove over to her place and pounded on the door, she didn't answer. And since he'd already given her back the extra key he'd had from Jake, he wasn't going to break in. Particularly when her toy car was missing from its usual spot in the shed.

He'd be damned if he'd chase around Weaver looking for her, though. He'd proposed to her, for God's sake, and she'd tossed it in his face.

So he went out to the Double-C. He found his father in the machine shop working underneath the ancient truck he was restoring. That wasn't surprising, but the sight of his grandfather sitting on a stool nearby was.

"Squire." He went over and shook the old man's hand. "I didn't know you and Grandma were back."

Matthew's voice came out from beneath the truck.

"Neither did I until I walked into the kitchen this morning and there he was, drinking coffee like always." He rolled out on the creeper and sat up.

"Your grandma was getting bored out in Arizona," Squire told him. He thumped the walking stick that was his only concession to old age. "Told her I liked looking at her legs in those skirts she wears on the golf course, but it didn't matter to her a lick." He shook his iron-gray head, a doleful look on his face that Derek didn't buy for a second. "Now I'm here watching your old man pretend to be a mechanic."

Derek hadn't felt like grinning since the worm had appeared at Sydney's place while he'd been chopping wood. But he did now. "*You* got bored, you mean," he corrected, and plucked a sugar cookie off a paper plate sitting on the ground beside Squire. He dunked it in the mug of steaming coffee sitting next to it and popped the entire thing in his mouth. It was warm inside the shop, so he dropped his coat on a workbench and shoved the long sleeves of his T-shirt up his arms.

"Man can only drive a cart up and down green hills so long," Squire admitted. He gave Derek a squinty-eyed look. "Hear you got yourself a girl again."

So much for Derek's grin. He shook his head. "Not quite."

"You keeping comp'ny with Jake's little sis or not? Heard you headed over there soon's you got back to town and didn't leave again even when the sun came up the next mornin'."

Derek slid his father a look. "That's what he hears, is it?"

His father shrugged, obviously unperturbed as he stacked two cookies in his fingers. "Stuff gets around, son. You know that."

Derek doubted that all of the "stuff" had made the rounds quite yet. At least he hoped to hell it hadn't. He sat on the bumper of the truck. "Sydney wasn't home this morning."

"It's Saturday," Squire grunted. "Women do all manner of stuff on Saturday mornings. Your grandma and ma are off shopping with your sister. Like it takes *three* women to find anything in Weaver."

"What're you complaining about, old man?" Matthew pushed his greasy boot against the base of Squire's walking stick. "So long as Jaimie brings you back some of Ruby's rolls, you're happy."

Squire contemplated that for about half a second. "True," he admitted. "You gonna marry the girl?" he asked Derek, not missing a beat.

Derek grimaced. "Hell, Grandpa, I just met the girl a few weeks ago." And she'd already made it plain she wasn't marrying *him*.

"Some of you young'uns are slower than others," Squire replied, looking slyly gleeful. "That whelp o' Jefferson's knew he wanted to marry our little Tara-girl when they first met."

Derek snorted. He knew good and well Axel and Tara's history. "They *met* about five years before they got hitched."

Squire waved that point away. "Just 'cause he was still a kid then. Had to go off and grow up some first so he'd be equal to the task."

Derek met his father's gaze and shook his head. Didn't matter what tack a person made, Squire was generally bound to take the opposite. He was just that way. "You want help with that thing, or you just gonna sit around and yak all morning with this guy?" He jerked his thumb toward Squire.

"Don't know as much as you think you do. If you don't realize by now, any time men stick their heads under an engine they don't need to stick their heads under, all they're in the mood to do *is* yak." Squire thumped his stick. "Hand me another one of them cookies. And then get whatever's stuck in your craw out so we can yak about that, too."

Derek handed Squire another cookie. "Nothing's stuck."

Squire harrumphed and practically swallowed the cookie whole, then leaned over and picked up the plate to balance on his knee. "Gotta eat a dozen of these dinky things just to get a decent-size bite." He gave Derek a look, his eyes paler blue than the winter sky and just as unyielding. "Never known you to be a liar, boy. Can tell just by lookin' at you, something's eatin' away."

"Nothing's stuck I can do a damn thing about," he said flatly, and pushed off the bumper. The truck rocked. He eyed his father. "You need help or not?"

Matthew pushed up off the floor and held out a long-handled wrench. "Get under there, then. Maybe it'll improve your mood."

Derek took the wrench and lay back on the creeper, rolling under the truck. But once he was there, staring up into the bowels of the Ford that had been old even when his father was a kid, all he saw was Sydney's pale face. Her wide eyes.

Where had she gone?

To see that slimeball she'd already wasted two years of her life with?

Derek made a face. He'd bet his own bank account—not nearly enough to buy even one of those ugly paintings of hers—that the guy'd never been flat on *his* back under anything greasy. For that matter, he'd probably never had grease on his hands at all.

And *she'd* chosen him.

But then he dismissed the idea that Sydney would even want to see the guy. He couldn't believe that of her. No woman was a good enough actress to convey as much loathing for someone as Sydney had for that bastard.

But she hadn't stuck around home, waiting for Derek's call, either, that's for sure. And she had to have known that he would follow through.

He pressed his boot heel against the cement and rolled out again. Sat up. Eyed the two men that had seen him through everything from baiting his first hook when he wasn't even school-aged to earning his third master's degree.

But he still didn't have any words to say when they all seemed balled up inside his chest in a god-awful knot. He shook his head, lay back again and rolled under the truck once more.

"He'll get there," he heard Squire say conversationally. "All you boys always do."

Derek set the wrench around a bolt and yanked, feeling the resistance all the way down his arm. He was glad Squire had so much confidence, because he sure in hell didn't.

"I appreciate you coming in to cover for me today," Tara was saying for about the tenth time, though she had yet to actually get out the door of the shop.

"I'm glad to do it," Sydney assured. "Go on back home. Get off your feet. Let your husband spoil you for the day."

Tara smiled wryly. "Axel's always trying to spoil me." She pressed her hand against her belly. "False labor pains. You just wait." She shook her head. "They're *such* a joy."

"You're sure they're false?" They'd been bad enough that they'd driven Tara to call Sydney that morning to come in and relieve her. "What if they're real?"

"Then I'll be needing you to cover for me more than I thought," Tara said, obviously unworried that would be the case. She finally pulled on her coat and headed for the door. "Don't forget. We close at noon on the weekends. Everyone in town knows it, and everyone seems to always wait until five minutes to, before deciding to come in and browse. They want something bad enough, they'll be back." She pointed her finger at Sydney as she went out the front door. "Noon."

Sydney nodded, though frankly she would have been happy to have the excuse of spending the entire day occupied at the shop rather than just the two hours that remained until closing. It was a lot better than sitting at home with nothing to do but think.

And wait for Derek to call. Or worse, come by.

She wasn't sure she'd have the strength to tell him no, again, if he climbed on his "willing to marry her" horse once more. And if she gave in to that, she'd be haunted for the rest of her days.

She didn't doubt that he would love her child.

But she couldn't bear it that he wouldn't love *her*.

Much better not to be at the cabin at all.

She hadn't even brought her cell phone with her.

No Derek.

Not today.

Probably not tomorrow.

Not until she got Antoine out of her hair and maybe, maybe, could focus on gaining some emotional distance.

She picked up her dusting rag and moved to the far corner of the empty shop where the children's section was and began working her way along the child-height display shelves. But every time she picked up a baseball glove she wondered, if her baby were a boy, how well he'd grow up without a father. And every time she picked up a lacy-dressed baby doll, she wondered how well her daughter would.

Sydney and her brother and sister had grown up with a father, unloving and distant though he was. And though she couldn't speak for Charlotte or Jake, *she* was a mess.

Maybe her child would simply be better off without a father at all.

Not if he were a man like Derek.

The little voice inside her head taunted her with the truth until Sydney finally gave up and moved from the children's section to the corner featuring women's clothing. But even there, she found a pretty maternity dress that stopped her in her tracks.

She gave up dusting and went back to sit behind the counter and fortunately, it was only a few minutes before she was relieved of her solitary, tormenting thoughts, when the door jingled cheerfully announcing the arrival of a customer. Unfortunately, the customer turned out to be three. Derek's mother. Derek's sister. Derek's grandmother.

Feeling as guilty as if she'd been caught standing naked in the middle of Main Street, she slid off the stool and smiled brightly. "Hello!"

"Hello, darling." Jaimie came right around the counter and gave her a quick hug and a kiss on her cheek. "You remember Gloria, don't you?"

Sydney nodded. "Of course. It's nice to see you again, Mrs. Clay."

Gloria waved that away. "Never got used to being called that even after all these years. Call me Gloria."

She had a ready smile as she headed toward the women's section that Sydney had just escaped.

"We're playing girlie-girls today," Sarah confided as she, too, gave Sydney a quick hug. "Manicures and pedicures over at Interludes. It's a new salon one of my friends has opened up on the other side of town." She tilted her head, studying the negligee on display inside the phone booth. "Appointments are at twelve-thirty. You ought to come with us."

Sydney opened her mouth to decline, but suddenly wondered why. Just because Derek had shown he had the sensitivity of a brick didn't mean she couldn't enjoy the company of these women, even if they were his family. "I'd love to."

Unlike Derek, who'd gotten his green eyes from their striking, auburn-haired mother, Sarah had gotten her pale blue ones from their father and now they were full of good cheer as she smiled. "Excellent." She was already pulling a cell phone out of her pocket. "I'll call over and let them know we'll be one more."

She started to move off toward her mother and grandmother, only to stop and reach into the phone booth to retrieve the negligee. "I think I'll try it on," she whispered to Sydney. "Donna Mae? Sarah Scalise here," she said into the phone as she aimed for the curtain-draped dressing rooms on the other side of the shop. "Got room for another when we come in?"

Fortunately, Sydney didn't have time to second-guess her decision. After the trio finished their purchases and headed to their next stop, making certain that Sydney knew where to meet them as soon as she'd closed up, a steady stream of customers followed.

And like Tara had said, several waited until the last five minutes. But unlike that day when Derek had wanted

Sydney to close early, this time, she willingly shooed away the browsers at noon. She locked the cash in the safe, locked up the shop and drove her car out from the alley where she'd parked.

She hadn't wanted to take any chances that Antoine might see it, if he was still hanging around Weaver.

She doubted it.

He was used to five-star hotels, of which Weaver possessed none, and since she'd told him she wasn't doing anything with him until Monday, he'd have probably sought finer accommodations elsewhere.

But she still wasn't chancing anything by parking out in the street where the car would have been easily seen by anyone driving by.

And that was also why she didn't take the shortest route on Main Street straight through to the other side of Weaver. The "new" Weaver, where Shop-World was located and multistoried condominiums and sprawling office buildings had sprung up, along with prettily landscaped neighborhoods lined with tidy houses that all looked the same.

Instead, she took the highway that looped around the town. And since it was the longer way and she'd have to backtrack several miles once she got off the highway on the other side, she drove faster than she ordinarily would have.

And it was only later that she knew she should have just chanced going through town.

"Put some back into it, boys." Squire was still sitting on his stool but Matthew and Derek had moved from working beneath the truck to working beneath the hood as they attached the hoist to lift the engine. "Never seen two men sporting my family name move so damn slow."

Matthew just shook his head and ignored the old man. "He's been off with Gloria for weeks," he dismissed. "So he's got a lot of mean built up in his system."

"Son, you don't know *mean,*" Squire put in.

"Was raised by you, wasn't I?" He looked back at Derek. "You got that side yet?"

Derek nodded and moved away to start jacking up the engine. It was slow work, but before long, the engine cleared the truck and they maneuvered it aside to attach to the engine stand. They were barely finished when the shop phone rang.

Matthew wiped his hands on the rag he pulled from his pocket and took the phone off the hook on the wall. "Yeah."

Derek knew something was wrong the instant his father's shoulders went rigid. His first thought was his mother. But when his dad's gaze turned on him, it wasn't anguish in them, but concern. "I'll tell him," he said, and hung up the phone.

Even Squire had risen. He clasped his hand over Derek's shoulder. "That was your mother," Matthew said. "It's Sydney. She's been in an accident, son."

Everything went still. "If that bastard hurt her or the baby, I'll kill him."

He saw the look that passed between his dad and his grandfather. But all Matthew said was, "She's at Weaver Hospital."

Derek was already striding out of the machine shop.

His dad caught up to him before he reached the truck. He grabbed the keys out of Derek's hand and shoved his coat into them instead. "I'll drive you," he said flatly.

Derek didn't care who drove, as long as they drove and drove fast. He headed around to the passenger side and swung up. Despite the grease on his jeans and his hands, he could smell Sydney's perfume and he clamped down on the ache that opened inside him.

In minutes, they'd left the Double-C behind and were flying toward town. "Your mom and Sarah and Gloria are all at the hospital already. Evidently they were at the beauty shop waiting for Sydney to join them when they heard about the accident."

Accident. His dad kept saying *accident*. "What kind of accident? How bad?" He couldn't think beyond that or he'd lose it.

"There was some sort of pileup on the highway, other side of town. Tractor rig lost a load of lumber. Pretty serious."

Derek had an instant vision of her small car going up against a steroid-size truck and his stomach churned.

"Your mother said she might need surgery. And miscarry regardless," Matthew added quietly.

"We need to get word to Jake and her sister."

"Your mom has it covered, Der. Don't worry."

He stared hard out the side window, wishing his dad would drive faster, even knowing they were already busting the limit.

"Anything you want to tell me before we get there?"

"Baby's not mine." He answered the question his father was really asking. He wished to hell it was. She wouldn't have had an argument against his proposal then, and he'd have been with her last night, and this morning, and if she'd had to be going anywhere—even the surprising girlfest with his mom—he'd have taken her. Or she'd at least have been in his truck. "If there still *is* a baby." He looked at his dad. "There's a guy. May be in town still, may not. Antoine son-of-a-bitch Kristoff. He needs to be *out* of town. Like yesterday."

His father's gaze slanted over him. "We got a legal reason to have him escorted away?"

Derek's jaw ached, it was clenched so hard. "Just that he'd sell his kid to save his own skin. I don't want him hearing about Sydney, or getting within twenty miles of her."

His dad absorbed that. Then he nodded once and urged the truck to go a little faster.

There were half a dozen ambulances jamming the emergency entrance of the hospital when they arrived. Derek jumped out before Matthew had fully stopped, and headed inside, working his way through the congestion of people crowded into the waiting area.

He spotted his cousin Courtney, who was a nurse there, calmly directing people from where she stood behind a desk. He rushed over to her.

Barely looking up from her clipboard and the frantic young man she was trying to calm, she pointed toward the swinging doors and said, "She's back with Mom."

Courtney's mother was Dr. Rebecca Clay. Considering she ran the entire hospital, Derek didn't know if the fact that she was treating Sydney was good or bad. He pushed through the double doors, looking right and left, not seeing anything but curtain-protected areas. But then he heard his aunt's voice right before two guys wearing blue scrubs pushed a gurney into view.

They were practically running.

And Derek's heart stopped dead in his chest at the sight of Sydney, pale as the white sheet beneath her, lying there. He broke into a run himself, but they were moving too fast, and his aunt caught his arm, dragging him to a stop with more strength than he'd have expected.

"You can't follow," she said gently. "She's going into

Surgery. She's bleeding internally and we have to get it stopped."

His throat didn't want to work. "She's pregnant."

Rebecca nodded. "We know. We're doing what we can." She nudged him out into the hall. "There's a waiting room outside of Surgery. You can wait there."

He didn't know where the hell Surgery was even located, but he nodded. "Take care of her."

She squeezed his hand. "We will, honey. You know we will."

And then she was gone.

All around Derek, nurses and white-coated doctors were running here and there, carting patients on gurneys and in wheelchairs, yelling at each other from one end of the hall to the other.

He heard none of it.

Because his heart had disappeared along with Sydney.

It was his cousin Courtney who finally noticed him, and directed him to the waiting room where his mom and the others already were. Courtney, who'd been called in because of the pileup, directed the rest of the family to the waiting room as well when they began to show up.

All of his aunts and uncles. All of his cousins.

One portion of Derek's mind had become aware of them. One portion of him appreciated their unwavering support, even though he knew they had more questions than answers about what was going on between him and Sydney.

The rest of him, though, could only sit there and exist through the minutes…then the hours…as they waited.

And waited.

And waited.

And even after the surgeon—some guy that Derek didn't even know—came out along with Rebecca to tell them that the first hurdle had been overcome…Sydney had lived through surgery…they had to wait some more.

Wait for Sydney to get out of recovery.

Wait for her to be moved to intensive care.

Wait. And wait. And wait.

And no matter how many times Derek asked to see her, the answer was always "as soon as possible."

As soon as possible came and went and went and went.

Tara was one of the first to leave but only because Axel looked ready to carry her out whether she liked it or not. "You call," she said. "The second you hear anything changes. You call."

He nodded. And after Tara, it was his sister. "I have to get back," she whispered, looking upset. "Megan and Eli have been alone all day. Max has been—"

On duty. That functioning, logical part of Derek's mind recognized that the sheriff would have more than the usual amount on his plate that day. He nodded. Felt her give him a hug. A kiss on his cheek.

And then it was Gloria and Squire. Neither one of them were up to spending hours on end sitting in a hospital waiting room. Derek didn't blame them, either. So it was more hugs. More kisses as they left, and were quickly replaced by his cousin Lucy and her new husband Beck—who was the son of Sydney's Aunt Susan's new husband. They had news that Jake and his crew would be there in a matter of hours.

He choked down some of the meal that his cousin Leandra brought by for everyone, only because he didn't want to have to deal with more nattering from his relatives, telling him he *had* to eat something.

What he *had* to do, was pray. And even though he wasn't exactly a churchgoing man these days, he went down to the chapel for a while and did that.

Close to midnight, J.D. and Jake and their entire crew showed up; they'd obviously come straight to the hospital from the airport. Maggie quickly stepped in to occupy their kids.

"What the hell happened?" Jake demanded as soon as the furor of their arrival died down. "My sister's pregnant? *Who the bloody hell's the father?*"

So Derek drew him out into the hall and filled him in. On Antoine, and his threats, at least. He left out the part that *he'd* been sleeping with the man's sister. And the fact that she'd kicked the idea of marrying him straight to the curb.

That was all still too raw for Derek to share.

Jake just shook his head. "I never could figure what she saw in him. Charlotte said once it was Syd's usual trick of finding someone just like our old man." An angry muscle flexed in his jaw. "There was no love lost between me and my father, but he was willing to buy off our mother to keep her away from us."

"Sydney's willing to buy off the worm to keep the baby from him."

Jake pinched the bridge of his nose. "She's not going to lose one thing to that guy. I'll take care of it."

"I don't know if he's even in town anymore. The family knows he's not welcome around here."

Jake nodded, needing no further explanation. He knew how the family could close ranks when they wanted. He looked at his watch. "Charlotte was going to try to get a flight back from Europe. I should be hearing from her soon."

"Jake? Derek?" Rebecca found them in the hallway. She looked exhausted. "Sydney is stable. She's not out of the woods yet, but it's a major step. You can come and see her, but only one at a time, and only for a few minutes."

Several of the others had come out to the hall, too, to hear Rebecca's report.

"I'll go," Jake said immediately, but J.D. caught his arm, holding him back.

"Let Derek go first," she suggested when Jake gave her a surprised look.

Derek felt the man's attention turn on him, but he wasn't interested in waiting around for what he did or didn't have to say about the matter. He was heading down the hall toward the intensive care unit.

She was lying in the first window-walled room he came to. A white sheet was folded over her up to her shoulders. Bandages covered her forehead. She was wired to humming, beeping monitors from both sides.

He was grateful there was a chair positioned just inside the open doorway, because his legs went out on him, and he would have hit the floor if it hadn't been there to catch him.

A moment later, Rebecca silently entered the room. She touched Derek's shoulder. "She's holding her own," she said softly. "I know she looks pretty banged up, but she's a fighter, or she wouldn't even have made it this far."

Derek had to clear his throat a few times before he could manage to speak. "What about the—" His throat closed again.

"Right now, *everything* seems stable," Rebecca said, understanding what he hadn't been able to ask. "That's all I can say for now." She nodded toward the hospital bed. "You only have a few minutes here, so don't waste them," she advised. "Talk to her. Hold her hand. Let her know we're waiting for her to come back to us." She headed out of the room.

He pulled the chair next to the bed. The knuckles on her hand were scraped, looking worse than his did from their contact with Antoine's nose. His hands shook as he cautiously slid his palm beneath hers.

Her skin was so pale he could see the blue veins running beneath the surface, and her fingers felt chilled.

His chest ached. "Come on, Sydney," he whispered. "You picked a helluva way to get everyone's attention." He brushed a lock of hair away from her white cheek. "But everyone's here. Waiting for you to open your eyes. Sunday dinner's gonna be here before you know it and my aunt Emily is cooking. She and Jefferson were here for a while, too. Said she expects you—" he had to stop and clear his throat "—expects you to be there with bells on."

The monitors continued to hum and beep.

He stared at her slender, scraped fingers in his. "And Tara," he added, forcing the words past the knots in his throat. "She's…looking forward to meeting that jewelry… dealer…you told her about. Says she's almost as excited about that as she is having you as a partner."

Hum. Beep.

He exhaled roughly. He didn't know how much time they'd give him with her. "Jake's here," he went on. "And your aunt and J.D. and little Tuck. Maggie's got Zach and Connor corralled in the waiting room playing games so they don't manage to blow up the hospital lab or something." He went still, imagining that he'd felt her fingers twitch in his.

But even as his heart churned, waiting for another tiny bit of movement, some show of life beyond the hums and the beeps of the monitors, she remained deathly still.

He could hear the nurses talking outside Sydney's machine-crowded cubicle and knew it meant his time was running even shorter. He pressed his mouth to the back of her hand. Willed some warmth into her. "Wake up and get stronger so you can get out of here and we can figure out where we're gonna fit a crib into that little cabin of yours."

"I'm sorry, Derek." One of the nurses peeked around the doorway. "It's time." She gave him a sympathetic look. "You can come back for a few minutes in another hour," she promised.

Sydney's breathing was so faint, he could barely make it out.

"Derek—"

He looked toward the nurse. "Come on, Theresa. We went to grade school together. Give me another minute."

"You put frogs in my desk," she reminded him softly, but made a face. "Fine. Another minute."

He leaned closer to Sydney, putting his mouth close to her ear. His eyes were burning. "Come back to *me,* cupcake. You don't have to marry me. Just come back."

She didn't move.

He swiped at his eyes and sat back.

Started to pull his hand away from hers.

But her fingers twitched. Definitely twitched.

He froze.

"Don't…call me…cupcake," she breathed.

Derek gave a choked laugh. Between her black lashes, he could see a thin glimpse of blue.

He leaned over her, careful not to jostle her, and kissed her lips. "I'll call you cupcake until you get yourself outta this hospital bed," he threatened.

"Odious man," she whispered. But there was a faint curve on her lips.

"I'll get the doctor." Theresa disappeared.

Derek curled his hand cautiously around Sydney's. "You're going to be okay," he told her. "Everything's going to be okay."

"What happened?" Her voice was weak. Barely audible.

The doctors had all warned that her memory might be sketchy on the details. "You were in an accident. It wasn't your fault and you don't have to worry about it. You're going to be fine."

Her fingers curled in his. Her eyes had closed again but a tear slid out from the corner. "I lost the baby."

He sat on the edge of the bed. Squeezed her hand. "No," he said firmly. "You didn't. You won't." Another tear trailed down her cheek and he thumbed it away. "You *won't,*" he repeated. Tears were burning out of his own eyes. "You're gonna be a great mom and that kid's gonna be a holy terror."

"Wish I'd been driving your truck."

He gave a broken laugh. "So do I, cupcake. So do I."

Chapter Twelve

"Please let me out of here," Sydney begged. It was Sunday afternoon. A week since the accident. A week in which she'd been moved from one section of the hospital to another. The latest was the obstetrics ward, though she was at the far end of the hall away from the hectic labor and delivery area. "I'm feeling good! Even the surgeon said he was satisfied with me."

Mallory Clay smiled wryly and continued studying Sydney's medical chart. "I'm starting to think you don't like our fine accommodations here, Sydney. You've been asking me to let you go every day for three days now."

Sydney plucked the thin blanket covering her legs. "I *have* stayed a few places a little nicer. At least ones that offered spa services instead of IV's and sonograms."

"Well." Mallory scribbled something on the chart and folded it with a snap. "Be glad for those sonograms we've been doing." She smiled. "Because that little baby growing inside you is looking pretty darn good and I *am* releasing you today." Before Sydney could let out a whoop, though, Mallory pointed the end of her pen at her. "But only to continue your bed rest at home."

Sydney nodded eagerly. "Whatever you say." She'd agree to anything as long as she was able to go home. "For, um… For how long?"

Mallory laughed softly. "Give me two weeks," she said. "That'll put you safely into your second trimester and then you can start getting back to your usual activity. Slowly." She jabbed her pen in the air, making her point.

"Slowly. I can do slow."

"That's what you say now," Mallory allowed. "But when I say bed rest for two weeks, that's exactly what I mean. It's not as easy as you might think. You can get up to use the bathroom, but that's it. On your back. No exertion. No activity. No sex."

Mallory was officially Sydney's obstetrician now. She'd seen parts of her that few people had, but Sydney still felt her face get hot at that last bit. "No worries there," she managed. The only man that would have involved was Derek, and since she'd woken up in the hospital with him by her side, she'd seen him only twice, and then for just a few minutes at a time.

It was from Jake that Sydney learned Antoine was well and truly gone. Bought off just as surely as their father had bought off their mother. Sydney hadn't had to use the agreement Brody had written up for her. She hadn't had to give up the Solieres. She hadn't even had to see him again. Jake had written a Forrest's Crossing check and now Antoine was gone and would never be back.

And while Sydney was relieved about that, it wasn't the subject of Antoine that had plagued her.

It had been the fact that during those few minutes with

Derek over the past week, he had made no mention whatsoever of what their future held. He'd only asked how she was feeling. Talked about how busy his business was getting since the G&G contract. Talked about the weather and the latest snow.

But he definitely hadn't talked about *them*.

Mallory had a faintly wry smile on her face again and was shaking her head as if she knew more than Sydney did. "No sex," she repeated. "Not for a while."

"I just had surgery," Sydney defended. "I'm not interested in all that, anyway." Which was a mammoth lie if there ever was one.

"You just keep that in mind." Mallory patted her blanket-covered foot. "One of the nurses will be by in a few minutes to finish up some paperwork with you and help you get dressed. And then you'll be able to blow this pop stand."

Earlier that week, J.D. and Charlotte—who'd arrived two days after the accident—had brought by some clothes and nightgowns so that Sydney didn't have to keep wearing only a hospital gown. She knew that there would be something in there that she could wear home from the hospital since the clothes that she'd been wearing when she'd been brought in by the ambulance had been ruined.

"Thanks, Mallory." Sydney really did appreciate the other woman's attention. She'd learned over the last several days what a stellar reputation Mallory had in her field.

"You're family," Mallory said easily as she headed out the door. "Don't forget. Straight to bed when you get home."

Sydney nodded, but she couldn't deny the excitement she felt knowing she was going to be able to leave the hospital. Knowing that she *and* the baby growing inside her were able to leave.

She let her head fall back against the pillows mounded behind her. She knew how very lucky she'd been. "It's selfish to want more," she said aloud.

"More what?" Charlotte came into the room just then. Despite being in Weaver where nearly everyone—even their brother, Jake—eventually seemed to succumb to the jeans-and-flannel route, Sydney's sister looked typically "Charlotte," dressed in a conservative gray suit with her blond hair pulled back in a sleek ponytail.

And seeing her now, Sydney realized just how much she'd been missing her. With Charlotte bearing the daily brunt of running Forco ever since Jake relinquished most of those duties to her, and Sydney's equally hectic schedule with Antoine, they rarely had found time for any sort of sisterly visit. "More…anything," she said now. "I could have lost this little one." She patted her belly. "But I didn't. I can't ask for more than that."

"Sure you can." Charlotte's eyes were full of humor as she settled her hip on the side of Sydney's bed. "You're a Forrest. We *always* ask for more. It's a family requirement."

Sydney smiled, too, but it wasn't as wholehearted as it should have been. "I'm going home today," she told her sister.

"Excellent!" Charlotte hopped off the bed. "I'll call Jake. I know they've got a room all ready for you—"

"*My* home," Sydney interrupted. "I'm going back to the cabin. I'm not staying with Jake and J.D." Charlotte was staying there now, but she was only going to be able to be there for a few more days before she had to go back to Europe to conclude her business that had been interrupted.

"I've seen that ancient little cabin," Charlotte reminded her. "It's hardly a place for you to stay on your own right now."

"It's perfectly fine!"

"It has *one* bedroom."

"I know that."

Charlotte looked skeptical. "Sweetie, you haven't stayed anywhere with only one bedroom…and one bathroom—a *tiny* bathroom, if I might add—for any length of time in your entire life."

"I am now." Sydney folded her arms across her chest. "You can't make me stay anywhere else. I love that little cabin. I'm fixing it up and I'm staying there."

"Well, slap my fanny," Charlotte drawled. "Aren't you getting to be quite the little stubborn thing?" But there was no meanness in her comment, just a sort of proud surprise. "So when can you leave? Anytime you're ready?"

"She can leave when she signs these papers." A nurse bustled into the room, her white-soled shoes squeaking on the floor.

Charlotte quickly scooted out of the way so the nurse could hand Sydney a clipboard and a pen, pointing out the places to sign. When Sydney was finished, she gave her a set of copies. "This last sheet has the date of your next appointment with Dr. Keegan," she finished. "As well as your instructions for continued bed rest. Now, I'll help you get dressed."

"I can do that," Charlotte offered, smoothly tucking the BlackBerry she'd been tapping on back into her purse.

"All rightee, then." The nurse smiled. "I'll get a wheelchair, and as soon as you're dressed, we'll get you out of here." She squeaked back out of the room, the forms on her clipboard flapping.

Despite Sydney's anxiousness to leave the hospital bed,

doing so took more effort than she'd expected. She still had a host of bumps and bruises, and she was stiff from head to toe. Fortunately, pulling on the pink fleecy sweatpants that Charlotte fed over her feet was fairly easy, as was zipping into the matching sweatshirt.

"I feel like all I'm missing are rabbit ears," Sydney muttered, as she gingerly sat in the wheelchair, "and I could play the Easter bunny."

Charlotte handed her the plastic bag containing the rest of her personal belongings and then wheeled her out into the hall. "Shut up," she said with sisterly ease. "You look fab in pink. Even pink fleece. I, on the other hand, look totally washed-out in it. And I *love* pink."

Sydney waved at the nurses at the busy nurses' station when they passed.

"See you in another few months," one of them called.

"God, that's right." They'd reached the elevator and Charlotte hit the call button. "You'll be back here when you deliver that baby. *Still* can't believe you're pregnant and you never told me."

She wasn't going to feel defensive over what was too late to be undone. "I was going to. I just wanted to tell all of you at the same time. Jake and Susan and you."

"Well, I'm going to forgive you," Charlotte allowed wryly, "but only because you're just getting out of the hospital."

The elevator door opened and Derek stood there.

Sydney's mouth went dry as she stared up at him. "You shaved," she said stupidly. His sharp jaw was completely devoid of the usual brown blur of stubble. And he had a cleft in his chin that she hadn't even known he possessed. He was also more dressed up than she'd ever seen, in black jeans and a white button-down shirt and a suede coat that was only a shade darker than the wavy hair that he'd ruthlessly combed back from his face.

Just looking at him made her want things. Impossible things. Forever things.

The corner of his lips kicked up. "Yeah." He gave Charlotte a little nod, but his gaze quickly returned to Sydney. "You're going home."

"How did you hear? It just happened."

The doors tried to close and his hand shot out, keeping them open. "Don't underestimate the grapevine."

"So, can I turn over wheelchair duties now?" Charlotte asked.

"I'm ready if you are."

Sydney looked from Derek to her sister and back again. "What's going on?"

"He's hijacking you," Charlotte said. "You won't go to Jake's. Fine. Then you'll go to Derek's instead."

Sydney's jaw dropped. "I told you." She sat forward in the wheelchair. "I'm going home. *My* home."

Derek's hand covered her shoulder, pushing her back into the chair. "You look like you're ready to make a run for it."

She couldn't have run even if she'd wanted to. She was feeling too off balance. Derek's hand on her shoulder, seeming to burn through her sweatshirt, wasn't helping any. His other hand was still keeping the elevator doors from closing on them.

"What did you do?" She eyed her sister accusingly. "Send him a text message on your phone?"

Charlotte lifted an unconcerned shoulder. "Like it or not, Syd, nobody is going to let you be alone right now." She crouched down next to the wheelchair and cupped Sydney's cheek. "You scared us all too much." Her voice was suddenly husky. "And much as I'd like to stay here with you—" she pressed her lips together, shaking her head "—I can't. Jake warned me to be careful what I wished for when it came to Forco. He was more right than I ever want him to know."

"But I've never even *been* to his place," she whispered, as if "he" weren't standing right there, hearing every word she said.

"I have more space than you do," Derek put in. "I'll be home with you at night, and during the day, either Susan or J.D. or Tara will be with you."

"Tara's ready to pop with that baby of hers." Sydney's nerves caromed about over that "at night" bit. "She, uh, she doesn't need to be worrying about me. I can't even help with the shop right now and—"

"Stop." Evidently tired of keeping the doors at bay, he pulled her chair toward him into the elevator and Charlotte quickly followed, so the doors could close. "You underestimate how much people around here have come to care about you," he said. "And Maggie's helping out at the shop again until you're back on your feet. It's already taken care of."

Her molars came together. The one person whose "caring" she wanted more than anyone's was *him* and he couldn't see past her pregnancy. "It's not up to you to take care of everything for me," she said, aware that Charlotte was listening avidly. "I'm not your responsibility."

"No," he said evenly, "you're a stubborn, annoying woman who barely got out alive after pitting her toy car against a semi, a ton of two-by-fours and two SUVs. *Indulge* me."

"Sounds like a good idea to me," Charlotte put in.

Sydney ignored her. Better for Derek to think she was stubborn and annoying than to realize she'd foolishly fallen in love with him. If he added pity to the mix, she wasn't sure she'd be able to bear it.

For that matter, she wasn't sure she would be able to bear being around him, anyway.

"The second I'm off bed rest, I'm gone," she warned flatly. "And that's the last of it."

Charlotte covered her mouth, muffling her laughter. "Oh, my God," she said after a moment. "You sound just like Dad. He always used to say that. Remember?"

Sydney glared at her. It was better than looking at Derek. Because when she did that, she turned into a bowl of mush.

The elevator doors opened, letting them out near the front entrance of the hospital. Derek left her long enough to pull his truck up to the front.

"*What* is wrong with you?" Charlotte asked the second he strode out the sliding glass doors. "That man didn't leave the hospital for one minute after they brought you in, until you regained consciousness."

Sydney's chest tightened. "He sure did leave quickly enough after that." Her fingers tightened around the plastic bag in her lap. "He only stayed long enough to make sure I didn't lose the baby. That's all he's doing now. Making sure I take care of myself because of the baby."

"And what's wrong with that?" Charlotte's eyebrows disappeared beneath the blond hair angled over her forehead. "You finally meet a man who's interested in—" she gestured "—babies and all that—something, I might add, that you've always claimed you *weren't* interested in—and you hold it against him?"

"He didn't even like me the first time we met!"

"Did you like him?" Charlotte shot back.

"He called me a snob." Her voice thickened. "And I called him odious."

Her sister was obviously amused. "Sounds like an interesting start."

Sydney, on the other hand, wasn't amused at all. She felt like her heart was in cold storage. Had felt like that for days now…ever since she realized that just because she'd awakened in that hospital bed to find him beside her, nothing between them had really changed.

"He didn't give two figs about me until he realized I was pregnant. I'm telling you, he's only interested in the baby." And as much as she loved her sister, she wasn't going to share Derek's reasons why. They were too personal to him. "If it were just *me,* he wouldn't give me the time of day."

"Well, sweetie, it isn't just *you,* and it seems to me he's giving you a heck of a lot more than a time update or a freaking fig tree. I wasn't here when they first brought you in, but J.D. says he was a wreck."

Tara had told Sydney the same thing.

But as she saw Derek's truck come to a stop outside the doors, she still couldn't let herself believe it.

"It doesn't matter." The words were as much for herself as they were for her sister. "We've only known each other a few weeks. Everything that's happened between us has been a reaction."

"Um…chemistry, maybe?"

Sydney was barely listening. She was watching Derek come around the front of his truck. He was holding a long, camel-colored coat in his hand, and she couldn't imagine where he would have gotten it.

Hers had been ruined in the accident, right along with the rest of her clothing.

"Never anything deliberate," she went on. "Never a *choice.*"

The glass doors hissed open.

Derek was coming toward her, his gaze on her.

"All right, then, if you had a choice," Charlotte said softly, "would you choose him?"

She had no time to answer her sister. Derek stopped in front of her and opened the coat, draping it over her legs and tucking it behind her shoulders. "I've got the heater on in the truck," he said. "But you need to tell me if you get too cold. Yes?"

Would she choose him?

Sydney nodded, answering Charlotte and Derek both. "Yes."

He took the handles on the wheelchair and rolled her through the door. When they reached the truck, Charlotte took her plastic bag and Derek simply lifted her from the chair to the front seat and made short work of pulling the seat belt around her and leaving the coat over her legs.

Aching inside, she let go of his neck, which she'd automatically clasped when he hoisted her into the truck. Charlotte got in the backseat but she leaned forward to whisper in her ear. "Never had a man carry *me* around."

Beneath the soft coat—and it was cashmere, every bit as fine as the coat she'd lost—her hands clenched together. Derek had carried her more than once, the night they'd made love. And it was more than a little shocking how thrilling it felt.

He climbed behind the wheel and she felt his gaze on her like a physical thing. "Okay?"

She nodded, swallowing past the knot in her throat. "Where'd you get the coat?"

"Picked it up yesterday in Cheyenne."

Her teeth found the inside of her lip. She felt Charlotte kick the back of her seat. "You…went to Cheyenne?"

He nodded and put the truck in gear, working his way

through the parking lot as if he'd had plenty of practice at it. "Had a few things to pick up there."

Which told her nothing. But the coat was truly lovely. "It wasn't necessary of you, but thank you," she managed. "If you tell me how much you spent, I'll pay you back."

His eyebrow rose and he gave her a slanted look. "I'll think about it."

Her fingers clenched together even more tightly. She turned and looked out the window and stared hard until she was certain she wasn't going to start bawling like a baby.

They quickly left the edges of town behind, but it was a while after that before Sydney realized they weren't heading toward the cabin or her brother's place. And both were on the way to Derek's home, she knew. "Where are we going?"

"It's Sunday."

She poked her hair behind her ear. It was getting long and needed a trim. "I'm aware of that."

"Dinner's out at the Double-C today."

"We're going to Sunday dinner?"

"Mmm-hmm."

Her stomach suddenly felt hollow. "But Mallory said I was supposed to keep off my feet. Bed rest."

"There're couches there," he reminded her dryly. "Mallory already knows we're going, anyway. She gave her official blessing."

Sydney pursed her lips and pointed her nose out the front window. Seemed to her that everyone was making a lot of decisions around her, and she wasn't sure she liked it at all.

"She used to pout like that when she was little, too," Charlotte said from her position in the backseat.

"Good to know," Derek said.

"I'm *right* here," Sydney muttered.

"And pouting," Charlotte added, laughter in her voice.

Someday, Sydney hoped her sister fell in love with someone who didn't love her back. Then maybe she'd have a little sympathy.

But as soon as she thought it, she changed her mind.

She wouldn't wish this much misery on her worst enemy, much less a sister that she loved.

Fortunately, Charlotte was good at filling awkward silences and she and Derek chatted away like old chums until they pulled up outside the Double-C.

"Stay put," Derek warned after he parked. He got out and Charlotte quickly leaned forward again over the back of Sydney's seat.

"If you don't want him, maybe I'll take a run at it."

Sydney shot Charlotte a deadly look.

Her sister just laughed, obviously satisfied with the reaction she'd gotten. "I knew it," she said, sounding superior. She pushed open her door and climbed out just as Derek was opening Sydney's.

"Good grief," she told him. "This place is *fabulous*. All this old stone work. I can't wait to see inside…" Her voice trailed off as Sydney saw her head toward the shallow steps leading to the front door.

As usual, her confident sister didn't wait around to be invited inside. She just marched right up the steps and through the door.

Derek was waiting.

And she was suddenly dry-mouthed all over again.

"Ready?"

She nodded and unclipped her safety belt, holding her breath as he lifted her out of the truck, keeping the coat around her as much as he could.

It didn't really matter. As long as he was holding her, she couldn't feel anything but the blazing warmth of him.

When she was clear of the door, she pushed it shut and then he turned toward the house.

"It occurred to me," he said, as he reached the first step, "that I didn't make myself clear last week."

She was holding herself as stiff as a poker, keeping as much distance between herself and him as she could, considering he had one arm under her leg and one behind her back. But it got even harder, particularly when he went up another step. She stared at his clean-shaven chin. "You've always been quite clear."

"No." He shook his head. Went up another step, jostling her just enough that she threw her arm around his neck to stay balanced. "I just didn't realize how unclear I had been until I saw you in the hospital." He went up the last step and crossed the wide porch, turning sideways to carry her through the opened door and into the living room.

She was aware of the crowd of people already there, but didn't think much of it since it was Sunday dinner and she'd already experienced what that meant to the Clays. Not until he carried her to one of the long couches that had obviously been left free just for her.

Everyone was watching them.

"I saw you in the hospital," he said quietly, "and I knew that if anything happened to you...*you*...my life would never be the same."

He set her down and tugged the coat she was clutching protectively against her out of her hands. He tossed it aside, and then he took her hands in his.

And it was only then that she realized they were shaking.

And then he knelt on one knee in front of her.

"You said that I'd never *asked* you to marry me." A muscle flexed in his jaw. "And technically, you were right. My mistake. But that never meant I didn't *want* to marry you."

"But that was just because of Ant—"

"Don't even say it," he cut her off. "That was timing, Sydney. That's all it was." He stopped suddenly. His eyes stared into hers and she felt the touch of them all the way to her soul. "What I realized in the hospital was that what I *should* have said was that I love you."

Tears suddenly sprang to her eyes. "Derek."

He squeezed her hands, warningly. "Let me finish."

She pressed her lips together.

"I should have said I love you. And I knew it when you were lying in that hospital bed, because if you hadn't made it back to us, you'd have been gone from me, never knowing that you had my…heart." His jaw canted and even through the tears blurring her vision, she saw his pain.

Pain she'd never even known was there. Just like the cleft in his chin. Because she hadn't seen past the surface. "Derek—" He squeezed her hands again in warning, and she fell silent.

Despite the number of people crowded into the room, everything was silent. Except the pounding of her heart inside her chest.

"And if I'd lost you," his voice turned raw when he finally continued, "without you ever knowing that—" He broke off again. Shook his head.

She couldn't bear his pain. She leaned forward, squeezing his hands this time. "It's okay. You don't have to—"

"I *do* have to." He shifted, tugging one hand free to pull something out of his pocket. "You have million-dollar paintings hanging on your walls. I can't ever hope to give you more of them. No matter what I do, how long I work, you'll always be richer than me. But what I do have, is this." He unfolded his hand, revealing a gleaming diamond ring.

The world seemed to shudder to a halt.

"I love you, Sydney Forrest. You *and* that baby you're carrying. I can't promise that we'll always agree." His lips twitched and he grinned crookedly. "In fact, I can pretty much promise that we'll often disagree."

She gave a faint, stunned laugh.

His grin died. His gaze didn't waver. "But I won't stop loving you," he went on quietly. "And I won't ever stop wanting to make a life with you. And I thought, maybe, if I admitted all of this in front of everyone who matters to us—"

He broke off to look around them and Sydney's bemused gaze followed. Jake and Charlotte and Susan were all there, too, standing arm in arm among all the others.

"If I did this with all of them here as witnesses," Derek said again, "maybe you'd realize that I am serious. And I do mean what I say." He held up the ring and the solitaire caught the light, sending prisms dancing around the room. "I love you, cupcake. *You.* And yes, that baby growing inside of you. So will you take my name? Will you hang your squiggly-lined paintings on our walls and stare down that sexy nose of yours at me when you're annoyed and teach our daughters how to throw rotten snowballs and—" He took a breath. His eyes gleamed like wet emeralds. "And wake up every morning next to me until I breathe my last?"

Everything inside her cried out *yes.*

"You said I shouldn't stay in Weaver."

"I was afraid you *wouldn't* stay in Weaver. But you did." His voice dropped to a rough whisper. "It took nearly losing you to make me face the truth. I don't ever want to let you go. Sydney, please. Will you be my wife?"

"You hardly spoke to me this past week."

He looked pained. "You're killing me here, cupcake. I had things to arrange. You think it's easy to make sure that every one of my family is in one place at one time? And that *your* family is there, too?"

Her gaze flicked beyond him. Even Mallory was there, even though she'd just been at the hospital. Plus more faces that she didn't even recognize.

"Come on, Sydney. How long do you want my heart hanging out in the open like this? I'm willing to let it as long as it takes, but if you're just gonna say no, then put me out of my misery and do it now."

She shook her head. Looked back into his face. She leaned closer to him. Cupped her hand against his smooth jaw. "You shaved because you wanted to propose to me," she murmured.

"It seemed like something you might appreciate."

"I do." She stared into his eyes, and knew, without question, that she could stare into them for decades and never tire of the view. Because his heart was there.

Right there for her to see.

As long as she looked.

"But I love you even with the stubble," she whispered. "I love you with grease on your hands and mud on your jeans. I love *you*." She sniffed and didn't care that her tears were falling. She didn't care, because she finally understood that with this man, she was always going to be safe. Loved. "And I want nothing more in this world than to spend my life with you," she continued. "To have your babies. To watch you teach our daughters how to throw a proper snowball and stand up for what they believe in and show our sons how to grow up to be as good a man as their father is." She held out her shaking hand. "So yes, Derek. Yes, I'll be your wife."

"Thank God," somebody muttered in the background and laughter started.

Sydney didn't care.

Derek had placed his ring on her finger and pulled her into his arms and as far as she was concerned, her world was complete.

"I love you," he said again. "I'm going to tell you that so often you're gonna get sick of it."

She tossed her head back and laughed, feeling more joy than she knew there was to feel. "We'll never know unless you try."

Epilogue

"Come on, cupcake. You're nearly there. *Push.*"

Sydney gritted her teeth and glared up at Derek even as she pushed for all she was worth. "Don't…call…me… cupcake…ahhhhh!"

"You're doing great," Mallory encouraged from behind her mask. Everyone in the labor room was wearing them except for Mom and Dad. "Come on now. Give me one more push and let's bring this little tyke out to meet you."

"I can't," she gasped. She was exhausted. Not sure she even had any strength left.

Derek pressed his cheek to hers. It was his strong chest behind her that had been holding her up for the last two hours of labor. It was his hands that were clasping hers, giving her something to dig her fingers into when the pain was nearly more than she could bear. "You can," he said softly. "You can do anything you put your mind to, Sydney. You're a Forrest and a Clay and neither one gives up."

"Next time we have a baby, *you* go through the labor," she panted.

He turned his head, kissing her cheek. His fingers threaded through hers again. "I would if I could, but I'm a bigger cupcake 'n you."

"Okay," Mallory warned. "Contraction coming up. Let's make it count, Sydney. You with me?"

She nodded, already feeling the building contraction ripping through her. She set her teeth, felt Derek's strength seem to flow through her, and pushed harder than she knew she could.

And suddenly, the blinding pain gave way in a gush.

"Thatagirl," Mallory crowed, bringing the baby up high enough for them to see. "You got yourselves a strapping baby boy here."

Sydney laughed weakly. Derek kissed her knuckles. Then her forehead. He was laughing, too, and she wasn't sure which one of them had more tears on their cheeks.

"You did it, Mrs. Clay." He kissed her hand again. "I knew you could."

"We did it." She lifted his hand and pressed her lips to the wedding ring that she'd placed on his finger only three short weeks after he'd brought her home from this same hospital after her accident. She'd been cleared of bed rest, most of her scrapes and bruises had healed and they'd gotten married right in the living room at the Double-C where he'd proposed. A more perfect wedding she couldn't have wished for.

"This little guy did some work of his own," Mallory interjected. She held up the squirming bundle of squalling little boy and set him on Sydney's chest. "May I present your son? All eight-point-six pounds of him."

Sydney's arms were so tired she was afraid she was going to drop him. But Derek was there. He'd always been there and she knew that he always would be. His arms surrounded them both, cradling the baby against her. "Our son."

"You're almost as beautiful as your mom," Derek told the baby gruffly. He rubbed his thumb over the baby's tiny, wrinkled forehead. "Don't know what we're gonna name you yet, but point-six is probably gonna stick as a nickname."

Sydney looked up at him, smiling. He still hadn't gotten over the value of the Solieres that even now were hanging on the wall in their living room. But he knew she loved them. And she knew he loved her. So he'd hung the paintings and added a few extra locks to their doors and did his best to forget they had a fortune on the wall.

She knew where the real fortune was.

And it wasn't in any squiggly lines on a canvas.

It was in the man holding her exhausted arms around their baby. His hair was a disheveled mess. He needed a shave and his green eyes were bloodshot from the hours spent ceaselessly at her side since bringing her to the hospital late the night before. He was the one who was beautiful and he was hers. "I love you."

"Not as much as I love you."

"Wanna bet?" Her racing heart was finally starting to slow. Mallory was busy down by her feet doing whatever it was that she did, and the rest of the delivery team was bustling around them. But as far as Sydney was concerned, her world just then was filled with only her husband and their perfect son. Her head found her favorite spot against Derek's chest. Where she could feel his heart beating behind her, and his steady breathing above her.

"I just pushed eight-point-six pounds of your son out of me and I'm ready to do it again just as soon as you are."

She felt the shuddering breath he drew. Felt the warmth of his lips against her forehead. "Maybe in a few years." His voice was husky. "It's going to take me that long to recover from all this."

"While you're scheduling out this young man's siblings—" Mallory came up next to her again "—I'm going to need him for just a few moments."

Sydney surrendered the baby and immediately felt the loss. She caught Derek's hands and folded his arms around her.

"What're we going to name him?"

For months, they'd been tossing around names. Since they'd decided not to find out the baby's gender beforehand, those names had covered the entire spectrum.

"He's Derek Jr.," Sydney said immediately.

"Nah. He needs his *own* name."

"It's a Southern thing," she drawled slowly. "Particularly with first sons. They're almost always named after their daddy."

"You don't have to do that. He's born a Clay, whether he's named after me or not. That's all that matters to me."

Sydney shifted around until she was facing him. She looped her hand around his neck and tugged his head toward her. "We're naming our son after the best man I've ever known. He's Derek Point-Six Clay Junior. We can call him DJ if you insist. But that's the last of it."

Bloodshot or not, his eyes filled with amusement. "Yes, ma'am." Then he caught her chin between his fingers. "And when we have a little girl, you're gonna let me call her *cupcake*."

She melted, already thinking of a little girl who'd have her daddy's eyes. "Anything that makes you happy."

His thumb brushed across her lip. "*You* make me happy, Sydney."

And then he kissed her, only stopping when Mallory noisily cleared her throat. She was cradling little DJ, newly swaddled in a blue-and-pink-striped blanket with a little knitted cap on his bald head. "Anyone want a baby here?"

Both Sydney and Derek's arms went out, and smiling, Mallory settled the baby into their arms.

And then, like the good and wise doctor that she was, she left the new little family alone.

* * * * *

Love Inspired®
SUSPENSE
RIVETING INSPIRATIONAL ROMANCE

Bakery owner Shelby Simons can't deny a stalker is after her, but admitting she needs a bodyguard is another issue. Bodyguard Ryder Malone is too big, too tough and way too attractive...but he won't take no for an answer. As Ryder and Shelby get close to answers—and each other—the killer closes in....

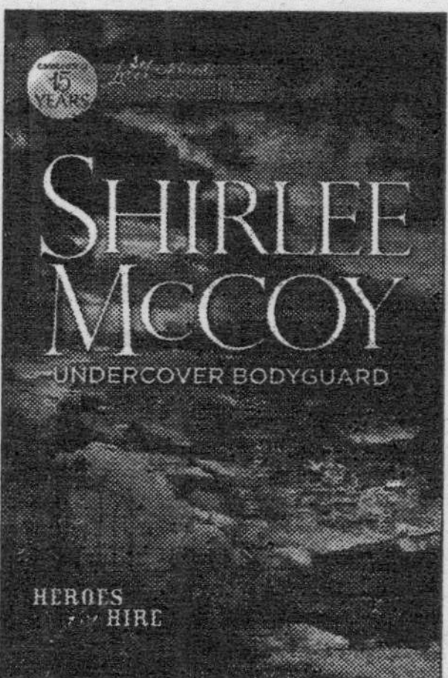

UNDERCOVER BODYGUARD

by SHIRLEE McCOY

HEROES *for* HIRE

Available April 2012 wherever books are sold

www.LoveInspiredBooks.com

LIS44484

PRESENTING...

More Than Words

STORIES OF THE HEART

Three bestselling authors
Three real-life heroines

Even as you read these words, there are women just like you stepping up and making a difference in their communities, making our world a better place to live. Three such exceptional women have been selected as recipients of Harlequin's More Than Words award. To celebrate their accomplishments, three bestselling authors have written short stories inspired by these real-life heroines.

Proceeds from the sale of this book will be reinvested into the Harlequin More Than Words program to support causes that are of concern to women.

Visit

www.HarlequinMoreThanWords.com

to nominate a real-life heroine from your community.

PHMTW769

get away from him.

Some part of him desperately wanted to think he had made some kind of mistake. It couldn't be her. That was just some other slender woman with a long sweep of honey-blond hair and big, blue, unforgettable eyes. But no. It was definitely Laura. Sweet and lovely.

Not his.

He was going to have to go over there and talk to her. He didn't want to. He wanted to stand there and pretend he hadn't seen her. But he was the fire chief. He couldn't hide out just because he had a painful history with the daughter of the property owner.

Sometimes he hated his job.

Will Taft and Laura be able to make the years recede...or is the gulf between them too broad to ever cross?

Find out in
A COLD CREEK REUNION
Available April 2012 from Harlequin® Special Edition®
wherever books are sold.

Celebrate the 30th anniversary
of Harlequin® Special Edition® with a bonus story
included in each Special Edition® book in April!

Copyright © 2012 by RaeAnne Thayne

HSEEXP0412

Taft Bowman knew he'd ruined any chance he'd had for happiness with Laura Pendleton when he drove her away years ago...and into the arms of another man, thousands of miles away. Now she was back, a widow with two small children...and despite himself, he was starting to believe in second chances.

Harlequin Special® Edition® presents a new installment in USA TODAY *bestselling author RaeAnne Thayne's miniseries,* THE COWBOYS OF COLD CREEK.

Enjoy a sneak peek of A COLD CREEK REUNION

Available April 2012 from Harlequin® Special Edition®

A younger woman stood there, and from this distance he had only a strange impression, as though she was somehow standing on an island of calm amid the chaos of the scene, the flashing lights of the emergency vehicles, shouts between his crew members, the excited buzz of the crowd.

And then the woman turned and he just about tripped over a snaking fire hose somebody shouldn't have left there.

Laura.

He froze, and for the first time in fifteen years as a firefighter, he forgot about the incident, his mission, just what the hell he was doing here.

Laura.

Ten years. He hadn't seen her in all that time, since the week before their wedding when she had given him back his ring and left town. Not just town. She had left the whole damn country, as if she couldn't run far enough to

Get swept away with a brand-new miniseries by USA TODAY *bestselling author*

MARGARET WAY

The Langdon Dynasty

Amelia Norton knows that in order to embrace her future, she must first face her past. As she unravels her family's secrets, she is forced to turn to gorgeous cattleman Dev Langdon for support—the man she vowed never to fall for again.

Against the haze of the sweltering Australian heat Mel's guarded exterior begins to crumble…and Dev will do whatever it takes to convince his childhood sweetheart to be his bride.

THE CATTLE KING'S BRIDE

Available April 2012

And look for

ARGENTINIAN IN THE OUTBACK

Coming in May 2012

www.Harlequin.com

HR17799

REQUEST YOUR FREE BOOKS!

2 FREE NOVELS PLUS 2 FREE GIFTS!

Harlequin®

SPECIAL EDITION

Life, Love & Family

YES! Please send me 2 FREE Harlequin® Special Edition novels and my 2 FREE gifts (gifts are worth about $10). After receiving them, if I don't wish to receive any more books, I can return the shipping statement marked "cancel." If I don't cancel, I will receive 6 brand-new novels every month and be billed just $4.49 per book in the U.S. or $5.24 per book in Canada. That's a saving of at least 14% off the cover price! It's quite a bargain! Shipping and handling is just 50¢ per book in the U.S. and 75¢ per book in Canada.* I understand that accepting the 2 free books and gifts places me under no obligation to buy anything. I can always return a shipment and cancel at any time. Even if I never buy another book, the two free books and gifts are mine to keep forever.

235/335 HDN FEGF

Name (PLEASE PRINT)

Address Apt. #

City State/Prov. Zip/Postal Code

Signature (if under 18, a parent or guardian must sign)

Mail to the **Reader Service:**
IN U.S.A.: P.O. Box 1867, Buffalo, NY 14240-1867
IN CANADA: P.O. Box 609, Fort Erie, Ontario L2A 5X3

Not valid for current subscribers to Harlequin Special Edition books.

Want to try two free books from another line?
Call 1-800-873-8635 or visit www.ReaderService.com.

* Terms and prices subject to change without notice. Prices do not include applicable taxes. Sales tax applicable in N.Y. Canadian residents will be charged applicable taxes. Offer not valid in Quebec. This offer is limited to one order per household. All orders subject to credit approval. Credit or debit balances in a customer's account(s) may be offset by any other outstanding balance owed by or to the customer. Please allow 4 to 6 weeks for delivery. Offer available while quantities last.

Your Privacy—The Reader Service is committed to protecting your privacy. Our Privacy Policy is available online at www.ReaderService.com or upon request from the Reader Service.

We make a portion of our mailing list available to reputable third parties that offer products we believe may interest you. If you prefer that we not exchange your name with third parties, or if you wish to clarify or modify your communication preferences, please visit us at www.ReaderService.com/consumerschoice or write to us at Reader Service Preference Service, P.O. Box 9062, Buffalo, NY 14269. Include your complete name and address.

HSE11B

HEART & HOME

Heartwarming romances where love can
happen right when you least expect it.

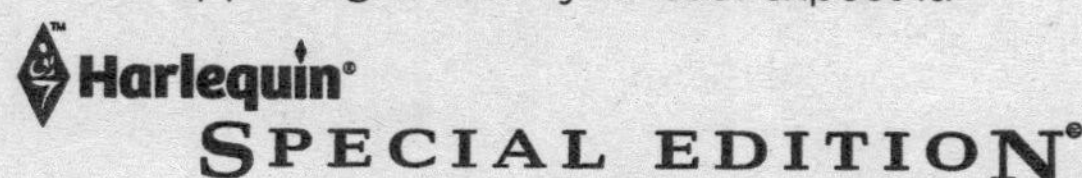

COMING NEXT MONTH
AVAILABLE MARCH 27, 2012

#2179 A COLD CREEK REUNION
The Cowboys of Cold Creek
RaeAnne Thayne

#2180 THE PRINCE'S SECRET BABY
The Bravo Royales
Christine Rimmer

#2181 FORTUNE'S HERO
The Fortunes of Texas: Whirlwind Romance
Susan Crosby

#2182 HAVING ADAM'S BABY
Welcome to Destiny
Christyne Butler

#2183 HUSBAND FOR A WEEKEND
Gina Wilkins

#2184 THE DOCTOR'S NOT-SO-LITTLE SECRET
Rx for Love
Cindy Kirk

You can find more information on upcoming Harlequin® titles, free excerpts and more at www.HarlequinInsideRomance.com.

HSECNM0312